Call To Murder

Behavorial Unit Maine Series Book Three

Bella Lane

Call To Murder Blurb

Escaped but never free. The phone rings, the hunt begins.

Kimberly "Kim" Santiago has been missing for a month, her sudden disappearance sending shockwaves through the FBI's Behavioral Unit of Maine.

When she reappears, she has no memory of the past month, but one thing is clear—the danger isn't over.

The real terror begins when the phone rings.

The person who took her isn't finished. He's calling her, taunting her, reminding her that escape was only the beginning. He wants her back, and he'll stop at nothing to reclaim what he believes is his.

Special Agent Declan Carr has spent the last month consumed with fear for Kim, not just as her colleague but as the man who loves her. Now that she's home, Declan is determined to keep her safe. But as the team races to uncover the identity of her captor, the threat closes in.

Can Declan protect Kim from a predator who's always one step ahead?

Or will The Caller come for her once more, to finish what he started?

Content

PLEASE READ CAREFULLY.

There are elements and themes within this book that some readers might find extremely upsetting. Please go to my website **www.be llalanebooks.com** under content warning for the list of potentially harmful topics. Please heed these as this contains some heavy situations that some readers could find damaging.

Table of contents

Chapter One

ERIC

"Kim," Michelle screams, catching Kim as she passes out while the tears fall down Michelle's face.

I dial 9-1-1, as I help Michelle gently lay Kim on the floor so I can assess her injuries for the dispatcher.

"9-1-1, what's your emergency?"

"This is Special Agent Eric Chandler from the FBI. I need an ambulance sent to the State Building Morgue. We have a forty-two-year-old female, who looks to have been severely beaten and is currently unconscious."

"At the morgue? No offense, Agent, but are you sure she isn't supposed to be at the morgue?"

"I'm sure. She's our missing agent and passed out immediately after arriving. Her pulse is low, and I need an ambulance now," I tell the dispatcher again, while trying to keep my composure.

"I have an ambulance on the way to you, Agent," she says as I hear her typing in the background.

"Can you tell me what her injuries look to be? Has she been shot or stabbed?"

"She's covered in bruises, dirt, and there is blood on her shirt, but I'm not seeing any gunshot or stab wounds to her abdomen or back," I relay to her as I continue checking over Kim.

I hear the operator type in my response.

"Her feet are bleeding and covered in dirt, like she may have been running through the woods. Her wrists have marks on them from possible restraints," I continue telling the dispatcher, as she continues to type.

"Agent, the ambulance has arrived and will be coming down the elevator momentarily. I apologize for misspeaking and pray for your agent's recovery," she tells me before disconnecting the call.

I quickly pocket my cell phone and stand up, walking out into the hallway. "The ambulance is here, love," I tell Michelle, raising my voice so she can hear me.

"You hear that, Kim, the ambulance is here to take you to the hospital. You're going to be okay," Shelly whispers to Kim.

The elevator doors open, and the EMTs push the stretcher out.

"In here," I call out to them as I walk back into the office. I lift Michelle up and away from Kim as three EMTs walk in.

I hold on to Michelle's shoulders, pressing her to my front as the EMTs assess Kim. I need to feel my wife, both to show her support and to help me focus on something else besides my failure as an agent in charge. I have failed Kim both as a boss and as a friend. She is lying on the floor battered and bruised, and we don't know how or why.

"Do you know what happened to her?" one of the EMTs asks.

"No. She showed up here like that and passed out. Never said a word," I tell them.

"I have a faint pulse, pass me the portable heart monitor," the EMT tells his colleague.

We watch as they attach the portable heart monitor to Kim.

"Hook an IV line up to her," the EMT, who's obviously in charge, tells his colleague, as he continues to monitor her heartbeat.

Once they have everything hooked up to Kim, they lift her and place her on the stretcher. We follow behind as they get her to the elevator.

Thankfully, the elevator is big enough for all of us. Michelle isn't ready to leave Kim yet and has her hand resting on Kim's.

When we get to the main floor, Michelle and I stay in the corner of the elevator, allowing the EMTs to go first with Kim. We watch as they load her up in the ambulance, before getting in my car and following them to the hospital.

I park in a spot labeled for law enforcement outside the ambulance bay. Michelle and I quickly run up to the ambulance as they are unloading Kim and follow them inside.

A trauma nurse rushes up to meet the EMTs, takes one look at Kim and says, "Trauma Two, what do we have?"

The EMT gives her a run down on Kim's condition as Michelle and I stand outside the room watching.

A nurse comes up behind us and asks, "Are you family?"

Michelle quickly responds. "Yes, and he's her boss," she says, pointing at me.

"Can you give me her name please?"

"FBI Agent Kimberly Santiago," I tell the nurse.

"Thank you..." She pauses, glancing between me and Shelly.

"Special Agent Eric Chandler, and this is Doctor Michelle Farrell-Chandler," I answer her silent question.

"The medical examiner?" she asks, looking at Michelle, who nods in agreement.

"I'm going to need you to fill out some paperwork while the staff works. Please take a seat in the waiting area, and once the doctor has seen her, someone will be out to talk with you," the nurse says in a soothing voice, with a small smile on her face.

Michelle takes the clipboard with the paperwork, turns, and looks back at Kim before nodding her head again.

I lead her over to some unoccupied seats.

"Are you going to call the team?" she asks while flipping through the paperwork.

"No, not yet. I want to see what the doctor has to say first," I tell her, running my hands through my hair.

"You should probably call Declan," she says.

"Why?" I ask curiously.

"He'll want to be here."

"I'm sure everyone will want to be here," I tell her.

"Yes, but he will need to be here," she says, looking pointedly at me.

"Is there something going on between the two of them that I need to know about?" I ask her.

I've had my suspicions, but it seems my wife may know for sure.

"Call Declan, please," she says before adding, "I'll call her mom."

I reach into my pocket for my cell phone and call Declan.

"Sir," he answers on the first ring.

"Declan, I need you to come to the emergency room at the hospital."

"Are you okay, Boss? Michelle?" he asks, his tone immediately changing from distracted to concerned.

"I'll tell you about it when you get here," I say before hanging up.

Michelle is on the phone with Kim's mother as she's filling out the paperwork that the hospital requires. Probably ensuring everything is documented correctly.

Twenty minutes later Declan shows up to the emergency room, looking around frantically and once his eyes fall on me and Michelle, I watch as his shoulders deflate with relief.

"Hey Boss, what's going on? Why are you and Michelle here?" he asks, looking over at Michelle and seeing we are both okay. I can see the confusion in his eyes when he looks back at me.

I take a long look at Declan and realize the man looks like hell.

"How much sleep have you gotten lately?" I ask out loud.

"I don't need to see a doctor, Boss," he tells me defensively.

"Hmmm, maybe, but that's not why I called you here," I tell him as I continue to stare at my agent.

He says nothing as he waits for me to elaborate. I look over at Michelle and see she is watching me. She nods slightly, and I take a deep breath before releasing it. I look back at Declan.

"Kim has been found, or rather she found us," I tell him.

"What? She's here?" he asks, his voice filled with hope. "Is she okay? Where has she been? Can I see her?"

"Calm down," I tell him. "The doctors are checking her out. She showed up at Michelle's office and then passed out. We don't have any answers yet, and we are waiting for the doctor to come talk to us. Declan, I have to tell you, she looks to have been really badly beaten. Until the doctor comes out, we won't know the extent of her injuries or how bad they are."

Declan goes pale, and I help him sit down in the nearest chair while he processes what I just told him.

"Breathe," I command as I continue to keep my hand on his shoulder.

I watch as he takes a deep breath, then another. Once the color comes back to his face, I lift my hand and ask him, "Are you good?"

He nods. "Yeah. I'm good. So, we just wait?" he asks, quietly.

"Yes," I tell him as I move to take my seat next to Michelle.

She grabs my hand and squeezes it before getting back to the paperwork.

After fifteen minutes she's finished, and I take the clipboard from her, walking back up to the nurse at the desk.

"Is there any news on Agent Santiago?" I ask as I hand her the clipboard.

"Nothing yet, Special Agent. Once the doctor has completed his exam, I'm sure he'll be out to speak with you," she tells me politely.

"Thank you," I say before walking back to the chair I vacated.

"Anything?" Michelle asks.

I can only shake my head no.

We sit in the waiting room for another two hours before a man in a white coat walks up and asks, "Special Agent Chandler?"

I stand up, as do Michelle and Declan. "Yes?"

"I'm Doctor Hunter Sava, I'm the on-call physician tonight."

"Please call me Eric. How is Kim?" I ask.

"Let's all take a seat," he tells us all, and we do. He sits in the vacant chair to the left of me, while Michelle is on the right side of me, and Declan is in the seat across from us.

"Agent Santiago has some serious injuries. We did several different scans that have revealed multiple broken bones, including her jaw, a few ribs, and her right arm. We had to wire her jaw shut in order to realign it, wrap her ribs, and place her arm into a cast. Her body is covered in bruises, indicating she took a severe beating for a long period of time. How long was she missing?"

"Almost a month," Michelle chokes out.

"Where did you find her?" Doctor Sava asks.

"We didn't. She showed up at the State Morgue, in front of Michelle's office," I tell him.

"Really?" he asks, shaking his head before continuing. "Your agent is a strong fighter. Between her injuries and the drugs in her system, I'm shocked to hear that she was able to move at all."

"Drugs?" I ask him.

"We did a blood draw, and the toxicologist identified at least two types of dissociative drugs in her system. They are still testing her blood to see if they can find anything else, so we know what we are working with," he tells us.

"What's next, Doctor Sava?" Michelle asks.

"We currently have her in a medically induced coma to allow her body to heal, but also to help get the drugs out of her system with as little side effects as possible. Unfortunately, I have no timeframe for you right now as to when we will try to pull her out. I need to ensure that the drugs are no longer in her system first," he tells us.

"Understood, Doctor, thank you for the update. When may we see her?" I ask.

"The nurses are getting her room ready, and as soon as she is set up, I will have the nurse come get you and take you to her room," he tells us, and we all nod.

He gets up and leaves the waiting area. I look at Declan and notice how pale he looks.

"Are you okay?" I ask him.

He can only shake his head no.

Michelle is silently crying next to me, and I wrap my arm around her, bringing her into my side while I hold her.

Twenty minutes later, a nurse comes to collect us. We walk down the hall to an elevator.

"Agent Santiago is in the ICU while she is in a coma," she tells us as she pushes the button.

We follow the nurse off the elevator, and she takes us down the hall to the ICU, past the nurse's desk, to a room on the right.

We walk into the room to the sounds of beeping. Kim is lying on her bed, hooked up to the machine that is causing the beeping sound. I know it's monitoring her heart and pulse, but the noise is already annoying. She currently has an IV line running from her arm up to two bags, presumably with antibiotics.

As the doctor stated, she has a cast on her arm, which is laid across her chest, and her face is still marred with bruises. Due to the blankets on top of her, I can't see the rest of her injuries, but thanks to the Doctor's update, we all know they are there.

The strong smell of antiseptic and cleaner hits me immediately, causing my eyes to burn slightly. The room itself is stark white, with a couple of chairs and a small sink attached to the wall.

Michelle walks up to the right side of her bed as Declan goes to the left side. I stand behind Michelle, watching her hold her best friend's hand.

"I can give you all five minutes, but then I am going to have to ask you to leave," the nurse whispers as she finishes checking Kim's vitals from the machine.

"That's not happening," Declan states with authority in his voice. "I'm not leaving her by herself, unguarded," he says, looking at me.

I nod. "Agent Carr will stay here with her," I tell the nurse.

"I'll have to clear that with the doctor and the hospital director, Agent," she says.

"That's fine. Let me know if there are any issues, but we will not leave our agent unprotected," I tell her, before adding, "Not after what she's been through."

She walks out of the room, and Michelle whispers, "Hey, sweetie, I know you can hear me, even if you can't wake up right now. I want you to know you're safe in the hospital, and Declan is here beside you. You have nothing to worry about except resting and getting better. We've all been so worried about you, but you are back with us, and we are going to make sure nothing happens to you."

The nurse walks back in and says, "Agent, the doctor and director agreed you can have one person stay with her at all times."

"Thank you," I whisper.

"Now, I'm going to have to ask two of you to leave. Visiting hours are from 8:30am-4:00pm, every day."

"Yes, ma'am. Come on Michelle, we can come back tomorrow. Declan, call me if you need anything or if something happens," I tell him pointedly.

"Yes, boss. Thank you," he says, looking down at Kim.

I lead Michelle out of Kim's room and back down the hall to the elevator.

"Do you think she will be okay?" Michelle asks as I push the button.

"Yes. She's a fighter, and she's going to want revenge on whoever did this to her," I tell her honestly.

"You're right," she says, taking a deep sigh. "When will you tell the team?"

"I'll call a team meeting in a few hours, but first, let's get you home and into bed. You need to sleep," I tell her, holding her close to me as we walk to the car.

"We need to find out what happened to Kim," she says, getting in the car.

"We will," I tell her, closing her door. "We most definitely will," I say, before getting into the driver's seat.

Chapter Two

UNKNOWN

Eight months before

I open the door to the bar, looking for a new victim. This bar is a popular place for women who come for after-work drinks with girlfriends and co-workers.

The ambience is light with plenty of booths, high tables, and bar seating. The bar top is a live edge maple wood, and the walls are painted dark gray with plenty of recess lighting, so the mood stays comfortable, but you can still see as you walk around.

I take a seat in a corner booth, hidden in the shadows. A waitress walks over to take my drink order. I order beer on tap, and when she walks away, I look around the bar, taking in all the women, waiting to see who grabs my attention. The waitress brings my beer, and I sip on it as I keep watch on everyone.

I watch a man with brown hair leave his friends and casually walk up to the dark-haired female at the bar. He leans over and says something to her that causes her to laugh out loud. Her laugh stirs something in me, causing chills to ride along my skin.

Yes, this is the one, I tell myself as I continue to watch them interact.

After a couple of hours of talking, they decide to leave the bar. I follow, neither of them noticing my presence. They continue chatting as he walks her home. I watch as they exchange numbers outside of her townhouse before saying goodnight. They don't even share a kiss.

He watches her go inside her home before he leaves with a smile on his face. No one should smile that wide, except me.

I take in the New England-style townhouse, knowing it won't take long for me to gain access. Walking around the side of the house, I see the entrance point I'm looking for-basement access. No one ever thinks about the basement. Getting into the house through the small basement window is not comfortable, especially for a man of my size, but it's still doable.

The next morning, I wait in the shadows of the buildings across the street for the woman to come out of her home. She's dressed in a black pants suit, with heels, and her dark hair is pulled back in a bun. I discreetly follow her as she walks down two blocks to an office building before opening the door and walking inside.

I check out the name on the door as I walk by *Largo Accounting/Tax Office.*

I continue on to the nearest coffee shop, knowing they will have Wi-Fi. I spend the day learning everything I can about the woman, starting with Largo Accounting and Tax Office and its employees.

When I go onto their website, I find her through a photo on their homepage. Her name and position are under her photo. It's like someone else did the research for me. Her name is Marabel Gonzalez, and she's the personal assistant to Jack Brown.

Having an account on white pages, and knowing her address, I look up her name, and there it lists her parent's names, and now I have her cell phone number.

Leaving the coffee shop, I walk back to my car. I drive to the next county, needing to buy a few burner phones.

That evening, I make the first call.

"Hello?"

"Anna?" I ask, knowing that is not her name.

"I'm sorry, but you have the wrong number," she says sweetly.

"I apologize, what is your name?"

"Marabel."

"Well, Marabel, you have a pretty voice. Do you want a friend?"

"Umm, who is this?"

"I would love to be friends," I tell her.

"I think I'll have to pass," she says.

"Want to play a game?"

"No, have a good evening," she tells me before hanging up.

"Ahh, sweet Marabel, I love games, and we are going to be good friends," I whisper into the dark.

I can't help the smile that crosses my face, knowing the game has started.

The next day, she leaves for work, and this time I don't follow. Instead, I walk to the side of her house where the basement window is. I pull my crowbar out from under my shirt and pry the window open. It takes me a few minutes as I'm sure she never opens this window and years of paint are making it difficult to open, but I finally get it loosened enough to push it open.

I squeeze my body through the tight window, only getting stuck for a few seconds. Once I'm standing on the floor of the basement, I close the window, knowing I won't be going out that way.

Finding the basement stairs, I take them up to the door that leads me straight into the cozy kitchen. The walls are bright white, with a huge window in front of me over a deep sink. The window is flanked by soft gray cabinets. There is a peninsula with cabinets below it, as it faces into the dining room that has a round table with four chairs around it.

Walking into the next room, which is a quaint living room, my vision is drawn to a wall of windows. Even with the shades closed, the room is bright. The furniture is nothing extravagant. Maybe some hand-me-down pieces that match the theme perfectly. Bypassing the front door, I go up the stairs where I know the bedrooms are.

The first door I peek into is her bedroom. It looks like she has a queen-size bed with two nightstands flanking it. On one of the nightstands is a photo of her with her parents next to the bedside lamp. The furniture in the room looks to be old and could use a good sprucing up.

Walking into her closet I see a wardrobe full of clothes and shoes that definitely don't look as if she shops at a thrift store, unlike the furniture in her house.

Making my way into her bathroom. It's a small room with a toilet, pedestal sink, and a shower, surrounded by older-looking tiles, but she seems to make it all work for her.

Reaching into my pocket I pull out my gift. I walk out of the bathroom, making my way downstairs to the fireplace in the living room and place my gift behind her photos on the mantle. As I turn, I catch sight of the cat before it darts underneath the couch. I chuckle as it almost made me jump, since I wasn't expecting it.

Walking back into the kitchen, I make my way to the back door. I unlock it before opening it, then quickly shut it, wondering if she will notice and think she forgot to lock it. I walk back around the house to the side where I entered from, checking to make sure there is no one around. When the coast is clear, I quickly make my way to the sidewalk and walk toward her place of work so I can continue watching my prey.

It's been two weeks since I began following and taunting my prey. She has yet to find the gifts that I have left for her in her house. Then again, I didn't make them too obvious when I visited her place, I've been there several times since that first day.

At twenty-five, she's single except for a cat and lives a very modest life. The only expensive thing she has is her wardrobe, and that's mainly for work. Her parents immigrated here from Venezuela, and she is the first generation in her family born in the United States. She's an only child who takes care of her parents as much as she can. One thing she does every week is spend Sunday dinner with them.

Saturday nights, though, are reserved for her friends and dates.

Watching as she leaves her office, she makes her way to the corner street, where she waits for the light to change, allowing her to cross the intersection.

I dial her number, which I know without looking as I listen for the ringtone and watch her pull her phone out of her bag.

"Hello?" she answers, her voice sounding so sweet and angelic, and yet, I can also hear the fear.

"Marabel," I breathe into the phone.

"I told you to stop calling me. Who are you? What do you want?" she seethes into the phone.

"Can we be friends?" I taunt.

"Why won't you leave me alone?" she whispers.

"Are you ready to play a game?"

"No, I don't want to play a game. I don't want to be friends. I want you to stop calling me and leave me alone," she says before disconnecting the call.

I chuckle, watching as she looks around before crossing the street and coming toward me.

Yes, soon I will have her. She will be a perfect addition, and I can't wait to break her.

I watch her as she walks past my hiding place. I can hear her erratic breathing, knowing she is concerned but not nearly fearful enough. But she will be soon.

She continues to look over her shoulder, and I hope she can feel me watching. I can't help the excitement that courses through me as I follow her home and watch her walk through her door. I know she thinks she's safe inside the house, but she'll soon find out. She is never safe from me.

None of them are safe from me.

Chapter Three

KIM

It's Friday evening, and we are having our weekly after-work drinks at McMillian's. I get to the bar a few minutes behind my best friend and college roommate, Dr. Michelle Farrell. She is currently the State Medical Examiner.

The waitress brings our wine, and we chat before the rest of the team shows up.

"What are your plans this weekend?" I ask Michelle.

"I have a conference to speak at in New York. I fly on the red eye tonight."

"You always have a conference to speak at," I whine a little bit, feeling like I never see my best friend anymore.

"I know, I'm sorry, but I promise we will take a weekend when neither of us has work, and we will book a spa weekend," Michelle tells me.

"I'm going to hold you to that." I laugh.

Just then, the door opens, and I watch as Heath, Mya, Frankie, Declan, and Eric, our boss, walk in and make a beeline for our booth.

My breath catches as soon as I see Declan. For almost twenty years, I have had a crush on this man, and as he gets older, he only seems to get more gorgeous. He's currently forty-one years old, standing at six foot one, his blond hair and gorgeous baby-blue eyes. I don't think in the last twenty years, he has changed a whole lot. His body is still fit and muscular, and when he smiles, his whole face lights up like a little kid at Christmas.

When he wears his suits, like today, he could pass for a GQ model. The women can't help but trip over themselves when he walks by, but he looks even better when he wears jeans and a t-shirt, well at least to me, he does.

Since the day we met, I've always felt an electrical current between the two of us. I've tried to ignore it and maintain a professional working relationship, but that's been hard. I'm not sure if he feels it too, since he's never given any indication that he thinks of me in that way.

The team walks up, and Eric stands at the end of the booth as he always does, never taking a seat. He only ever has one drink with the team and then leaves, so I expect nothing different from him tonight either.

Heath slides in beside Michelle, with Mya squeezing next to Heath. I notice Frankie stops at the bar, striking up a conversation with a female sitting there. Declan takes the seat beside me, his leg brushing up against mine, causing an electric current to run through my body.

I can't help the moan that escapes me but quickly cover it by taking a sip of my wine.

As a team, we made a rule that there would be no inner dating to avoid disrupting the team dynamic, but I don't know how much longer I can go on pretending–especially when he is sitting so close to me, as he is right now.

I can feel the warmth from his body seeping into me as it surrounds me like the sunshine beating down on a perfect spring day. I inhale his earthy and woodsy scent, reminding me of the outdoors and our time spent at the lake.

I get pulled out of my thoughts about Declan when I hear Heath ask a question.

"What are we talking about?" Heath asks, just as the waitress comes up to take everyone's order. Both Michelle and I get a refill on our glasses of wine.

Once the waitress leaves to get everyone's order, I answer Heath.

"We were discussing Shelly's conference this weekend in New York."

"You're leaving again?" Heath looks at her with a pout.

"Yes," she answers with a chuckle. "I have to give a lecture during the conference this weekend."

"You are always working, you need to make time to play," Heath tells her.

"I said the same thing," I tell him with a small smile on my face as Declan's hand brushes up against my thigh.

"Well, what are you doing this weekend?" Shelly asks Heath as I try to maintain my composure.

"You mean who, and I haven't decided yet," he says, a sneaky gleam in his eyes.

Shelly and I both roll our eyes as the waitress brings everyone's drinks.

"Actually, I was thinking we could all go to the cabin this weekend," Heath says nonchalantly.

"You know it's too cold to go into the lake, right?" I tell him.

"I know that, but that doesn't mean we can't do some hiking and sit around the firepit," he says, whining a little bit.

"So, you're dateless this weekend?" Declan quips.

Normally, Heath only wants to hang out when he doesn't have a man to spend time with, though I never really mind. Heath has become another girlfriend and usually hangs out with Michelle and I often.

"I'll be happy to go to the cabin with you this weekend," I tell Heath with a smile.

"Yeah, I'll go too. Hiking sounds exactly like what I need," Declan says, surprising me.

"Sorry, but I'm going to have to pass this weekend," Mya says.

"Oh, why is that? Do you have a mystery date?" Heath asks.

Mya shakes her head no, but doesn't elaborate any further.

Frankie finally comes over to join us, and he sits down next to Declan.

"What did I miss?" he asks.

"We are talking about going to the cabin this weekend and doing some hiking," Heath says, then asks, "Did you get her number?"

We all look at Frankie, who actually blushes a little before he says, "Nah, apparently, my pickup line wasn't as good as the guy's next to her."

"What did you say?" Heath asks.

"I asked her if she liked to dance, and she said yes and truly looked excited and interested," he tells us.

"Then what did you say?" Heath asks, knowing something Frankie said killed it.

"I asked if I could show her my horizontal mambo moves," he says with a shrug of his shoulders.

"Oh my God," Shelly says.

"No, you didn't," I say at the same time.

"That right there is why you will be spending the weekend hiking with us," Heath says, sounding exasperated. "I mean, I'm gay, and I know you don't say anything like that to a woman. You should have asked if you could take her dancing, then later, after showing her a good time, if things were going well, then bring that up."

"I don't understand. I thought women wanted honesty?" Frankie says, looking perplexed.

"We do, but we also want to be wooed," Mya tells him before taking a sip of her drink.

"A decent woman is not going to fall into your bed right away," Shelly begins. "She wants to know that you are really interested in her and not just for sex. Women like to get to know men and hope that men want to get to know them too," Shelly tells him.

"Do you want a relationship?" Heath asks him.

I can see Frankie glance over at me from the corner of my eye, but I sip my wine, pretending not to notice.

"Eventually. I'm hoping the right one will want me," Frankie responds, as he looks back at his beer.

"Then you need to work on how to interact with women, my friend," Heath says before adding, "Or you are going to be a one-fisted man for the rest of your life."

We all just shake our heads but can't help the chuckles that leave our lips.

"I'm trying, it's just so hard," Frankie whines.

"Just remember the things we've told you in the past, and get out of your head," I tell him, hoping to soften the blow.

I know Frankie is hoping that I'll be his one and only, but I feel nothing except sisterly toward him. He doesn't make my body simmer as Declan does, but I also know even without our internal rule, Frankie and Declan are friends, and that in itself could cause major problems.

"Man, if you're interested in someone, ask them to dinner, find out what they like, don't like. You are an FBI agent, use your interrogation skills. Go out more than once, doing things you both like," Declan tells Frankie.

"When's the last time you were on a date?" Frankie asks him pointedly.

"Good point," Declan says before taking another sip of his drink.

"Well, as fun as this has been, I need to get home and pack before my flight," Shelly says.

"I would say have fun, but there is no way those conferences are fun, so I will say, don't do anything I wouldn't do," Heath tells Shelly.

"What wouldn't you do?" Shelly asks, laughing.

"Nothing, because I do everything," he replies with a wink as he and Mya slide out of the booth to let Shelly out.

"Be safe, Shelly, and call me when you're back," I call out to her, and she waves.

"I need to get going too," Mya says.

"Let's walk out together. I want to check out that piece over by the door, but I don't want to make it obvious." Heath says, looping his arm through Mya's as they head for the door.

"Good night you two," I say as I chuckle.

Heath turns back around and says, "Let's meet up at ten am tomorrow."

"Okay," Declan and I say at the same time.

"I'm going to get another drink. Do either of you want one?" Frankie asks.

"No, I think I'm going to head home as well," I say as I finish my last little bit of wine.

"Yeah, none for me either man, I'm going to head home too. It's been a long week," Declan says.

"That's true, but I'm going to grab another drink before I head home. See you both tomorrow," Frankie says as he slides out of the booth and makes his way to the bar.

I set my glass on the table, waiting for Declan to slide out.

"Want to go grab something to eat?" Declan asks, and I look over at him, making sure he is talking to me.

"I'm sorry, are you asking me?" I ask him.

"Yes, but if you prefer not to or would rather have Frankie join us, I can ask him," he says, with a frown on his face and sounding unsure of himself.

"No," I say quickly before taking a deep breath. "Yes, I would love to grab something to eat, and no, you don't need to ask Frankie to come," I elaborate.

He shoots me his blinding smile, and thank goodness I'm still sitting down, otherwise my legs would have given out from underneath me.

"Do you have anything special in mind?" he asks me, and I can only shake my head no. "I know this pretty good Mexican restaurant if you would like to go there?"

"That sounds good," I say breathlessly.

Declan finishes his drink and then slides out of the booth. I follow him out, and then we both wave goodbye to Frankie, who is sitting next to a female at the bar.

Walking outside the bar and onto the sidewalk, Declan looks at me and says, "Do you want to follow me over there?"

"Sure," I respond as I walk to my car.

Once in, I take a deep breath, "Get it together, Kim. This could just be dinner with a colleague since he was willing to invite Frankie. Maybe he doesn't want to eat alone," I tell myself as I follow behind Declan to the restaurant.

Surprisingly, the restaurant is in my neighborhood, and it's the only one I haven't visited yet. I park the car and take a deep breath to calm my heart rate.

My door opens, and I squeal, "EEK!"

"I'm..I'm..sorry," Declan stammers, "I thought I would be nice and get your door."

With my hand on my heart, I tell him, "It's fine, just not something I was expecting."

He holds his hand out to help me out of the car, and I can't help but jump at the opportunity to touch him.

As soon as our hands touch, I feel an electric shock all the way to my core. I can't help but moan, though I try to cover it with a cough.

"Thank you," I say as I look up at him.

I can see heat and desire shining back at me through his eyes, and my breath gets caught in my throat. His eyes dip down to my lips, and I immediately lick them, knowing they are dry right now.

I hear him give a little moan as he shakes his head slightly and closes my car door.

I quickly lock it as he continues holding my hand and leads me to the front of the restaurant.

Once inside, the hostess greets us, "Good evening, just two?"

"Yes, please," Declan says, still not letting go of my hand.

I take in the quaint ambiance of the restaurant. It's not big by any means, with a few booths alongside a wall of windows. There are a few tables and chairs next to a side brick wall, wood floors running throughout, and the murals on the walls are bright and colorful, making the place feel warm and inviting.

There is a bar on the other side of the room, showcasing different alcohols on a wall of shelves across that brick wall. Strings of lights are hung across the restaurant in different colors. The back wall leading to the kitchen is painted a vibrant blue, giving off fun vibes in the place.

We are led to a corner table at the back of the restaurant. Declan lets go of my hand, and I can't help but feel like I just lost a part of myself. I shake my head as I slide into the chair that he is holding out for me before taking a seat in the chair across from me.

"What can I get you to drink?" she asks.

"Water with lemon, please," I tell her.

"I'll have the same, and could we also get the Queso Fundito?" Declan asks her.

"Would you like any meat with that?"

"No, thank you," Declan tells her.

"No problem. I'll be right back with your drinks and Queso Fundito," she says before walking away.

I look at the menu that she placed on the table in front of me to see what Queso Fundito is. Reading the description, I see it's melted queso chorizo, queso fresco, pickled jalapeños, pico de gallo, and salsa roja served in a hot skillet with a side of chips.

Sounds delicious, I think to myself as I continue looking over the menu. "So, what is good here?" I ask Declan, already knowing this isn't his first time here.

"Everything, if I'm being honest," he tells me, not even looking at his menu.

"Hmmm," I say as I continue perusing.

The waitress comes back with our waters and Queso Fundito, which looks great.

"Are you ready to order?" she asks.

Declan and I both nod, and he says, "Go ahead."

"Can I get your enchiladas with chicken, please?"

"What choice of sauce would you like? Salsa roja, salsa verde, or queso sauce?"

"Salsa verde, please," I tell her before placing my menu at the edge of the table.

"And for you, sir?"

"I would like two of your carne asada puffy tacos, please, and make it a meal," Declan tells her.

"And would you like your enchiladas a meal as well, ma'am?" she asks me.

I must look confused because then she adds, "A meal consists of rice, beans, and a side salad."

"Yes, please," I tell her. "I'm sorry, I thought it was all-inclusive."

I'm used to DC, all the Mexican restaurants there when you order, the sides are automatic, but good to know for the next time I come here.

She takes our menus and walks away. I grab a chip and try the Queso Fundito as Declan watches me. Once the taste hits my tongue, I feel like I'm transported back to my time in Mexico when I went to visit family.

"Wow, this is really good," I tell him, getting another.

"Yeah," he says with a smile. "It was a fluke that I found this place. I was driving around, and it caught my eye. Now when I want Mexican, this is the place I come to," he informs me.

We sit in silence, eating the Queso Fundito and drinking our waters. It's not an overbearing silence, but I wish I knew what was going on in his mind right now. Then, as if he could read my mind.

"How long have we worked together?" Declan asks.

"A long time," I say, wistfully. "Almost twenty years, I think," I add as I take a long drink of my water.

He nods, "I think it's time we address this thing between us," Declan says, and I immediately choke on my water, not expecting those words.

Chapter Four

DECLAN

"Are you okay?" I ask her.

"Yeah, I'm good," she says as she catches her breath.

"I didn't mean to make you choke," I tell her.

"I just wasn't expecting that."

"I probably could have said it a different way, but tell me, am I the only one who feels this pull between us?" I ask, needing to know and hoping I'm not wrong.

She shakes her head. "No, you're not, but it's not about us," she says softly.

"I know we set the rule so as not to disrupt the team dynamic. I thought at first it was just an infatuation that would go away, but over the years, that pull has become stronger, at least for me anyway." I say the last part in a whisper while looking down at the table.

"It has for me as well," she says. "But this isn't just about us. Frankie has made his feelings and intentions toward me very clear," she starts.

"Do you have feelings for him?" I interrupt, needing to know.

Frankie has already told me several times how he feels about Kim, but I need to know if she feels the same way.

"No," she says, looking at me, shocked. "Not in a romantic way. He's almost like the little annoying brother that I never wanted but would still protect if needed."

I laugh out loud because that sounds about right when it comes to Frankie. He's only been with the team for the last ten years and is currently the youngest on the team, as Mya is a year older than him. He is always putting his foot in his mouth, especially when it comes to females, though he is a great FBI agent, and would do anything for anyone if they asked.

"I understand," I say as the smile spreads across my face.

The waitress walks up to our table and places our food down in front of us.

"Can I get you anything else?" she asks.

"Some more water, please," I respond.

"Absolutely," she beams as she walks away.

I watch as Kim looks down at her plate.

The waitress comes back with a pitcher of water and fills our glasses up. "Let me know if you need anything else," she says before walking away again.

"Wow, this is a lot of food," Kim mutters.

I chuckle as I dig into my puffy taco.

I watch as she takes a bite of her enchilada and see the surprise flitter across her face. "Do you like it?" I ask.

"I do. This is very authentic and wonderful," she tells me before placing her fork down and looking up at me with beautiful, deep brown eyes. She takes a deep breath and then says, "Though I may not have feelings for Frankie, the fact is he thinks he does. You two have been friends for a long time. I won't lie and say I haven't thought about there being an us, but it would cause more problems, not just for the team itself but between you and Frankie, which could also cause issues between Frankie and myself. Wow, what a mess," she tells me.

I place my taco on the plate, knowing what she is saying is right, but it's not what my heart wants to hear.

"So, you've thought about us?" I ask.

I watch as she puts her hand over her mouth like she just let the biggest secret out.

"I admit, I've thought about us over the years as well. To be honest, that's how I found this place," I tell her and see the confusion all over her face.

"When we were in DC, I used to drive by your place, trying to work up the courage to knock on your door, then when we moved here, I did the same. When I found this place, I'd just tell myself I wanted Mexican, but I can't keep pretending I don't want you, Kim. If need be, I'll transfer back to DC, but I don't want to continue as if I don't feel something for you. I want to explore this and see where it goes."

"What if it goes nowhere?" she whispers. "What if the dreams don't live up to reality, and we only end up hurting each other?"

"We can play the what-if game all night. What if we are soulmates, meant to spend eternity together, and yet we keep letting the years go by, doing nothing? We aren't getting any younger, Kim. Look at the years we have already wasted by not being honest. It's been almost twenty years." I implore her to see reason.

"You're right," she says, shocking me. "We have wasted a lot of years already, but I don't want you to go back to DC."

"How can we make this work?" I ask.

"I'm not keen on the prospect of long distance to start with. Maybe we can keep this quiet from the team and see how things go between us before we make any permanent decisions about our careers," she offers.

I mull over what she says, and though I'm not excited about the secrecy, I understand what she is saying. "Okay, we can try this out your way," I tell her as I grab and hold her hand, feeling the electric current run between the two of us.

I watch as she smiles big and bright, causing my heart to sputter from her beauty and my cock to harden. It takes everything in me to allow us both to finish eating, when all I want to do is pull her on top of me and ravish her body.

Once we are done, I pay the bill, and then lead us out to the parking lot. Standing next to her car, I lean down and kiss her lips. I always imagined they would be soft, but the reality is so much better.

She sighs, giving me the access I need to swipe my tongue in her mouth and deepen the kiss. Our kiss turns into a frenzy, and I know I need to pull away before I undress her here in the parking lot.

Reluctantly, I pull back and break the kiss. Her lips are swollen, her cheeks are flushed, and she looks like a goddess.

"We should probably stop before the cops show up and get us for indecent exposure," I say with a little smile, and she laughs.

I love the sound of her laugh, it feels like home.

"Want to come over to my place and have some coffee?" she asks, shyly.

"I would love to," I tell her. "I'll follow you," I add before opening her car door and waiting for her to get in, then closing it.

I get in my car and start it, ready to follow her home, hell to the ends of the earth if that's what it takes. I've been in love with Kim for almost twenty years since the first day I laid eyes on her. I knew she was the one for me, but I didn't want to hurt my chances of being on the team, so I pretended every day that there was nothing there.

Sure, I dated a few women, but they weren't Kim, so the relationships never lasted long. I never married or had kids because there was only one woman I wanted all that with, and she was out of my reach, or so I thought.

That was when I realized I'd been content sitting on the sidelines, wanting and waiting. Spending time with my siblings and their families over the Labor Day weekend, it hit me, what was I waiting for? Life was passing me by, and I was doing nothing about it.

Sitting in the booth, next to Kim, feeling the electrical current between us, and hearing her moan slightly when I touched her, I knew it was time to make my move. I didn't expect her to suggest a secret romance, and I'm not thrilled with the prospect of keeping secrets from our co-workers, but I also understand why. I just hope we don't have to be secret for a long time.

I follow her the short distance to her house and park my car behind hers in her driveway. We both get out of our cars at the same time and walk up the sidewalk to the front door. She places her key in the lock and opens the door. I wait for her to walk into her home first before I follow behind her.

She places her keys and phone on the console near her door, taking her shoes off by the door. I follow her lead, taking my shoes off as well, before following her down the hall and into the kitchen.

Her kitchen is open to the living and dining room with a huge island. Instead of a dining table, she has her gym equipment, where she must workout. She has hardwood floors that run throughout the main living area.

I watch as she walks over to the coffee pot. She reaches up to the cabinet, but instead of opening it, she turns and walks over to me. She reaches up and places both hands on the side of my face, pulling me toward her as she leans up and slams her lips on mine.

This time, she managed to shock and surprise me. She pulls back and says, "I don't really want coffee, do you?"

I can only shake my head no as she pulls my hand and leads me to a door off the living room. When we walk in, I see this must be her bedroom. Before I have time to get my bearings, Kim reaches up and begins to unbutton my shirt. She slides the shirt off my shoulders and down my arms, leaving it on the floor.

I lean down, taking her lips with mine, as I unbutton her shirt, needing to feel her skin with my hands. I send her shirt to the floor with mine and begin to unbutton her pants. I pull them down her legs and help her step out of them before I stand back and admire the woman in front of me.

Kim Santiago is standing in front of me with only a white lacy bra and panty set covering her. The white is bright against her dark, tanned skin. Her body is slender and toned, her stomach flat, and her breasts fill her bra cup perfectly. I kiss her neck, reaching around to undo her bra, needing to touch, squeeze, and taste her breasts.

As soon as the bra is out of the way, I latch my mouth to one of her nipples as if I'm a starving infant looking for nourishment while I knead the other with my hand. So many nights I dreamed about this, woke up hard with the need for this gorgeous woman. I'm just praying this isn't a dream, too. I pinch her nipple and hear her gasp and moan at the same time.

I feel her hands in my hair as she tugs, letting me know this is real and not a dream. I bend down and pick her up by her legs, wrapping them around my waist as I lead us both to her bed, where I lay her down gently.

I cup her pussy, sliding my finger under her lacy panties, and thrust it inside her. Her back bows up. I lean over her, taking her nipple in my mouth and sucking while I add another finger inside her.

She starts riding my fingers, chasing her release. I pull my fingers out, grabbing her panties and slide them down her legs. I spread her legs open and allow my eyes to feast on her swollen, dripping, pink pussy.

I spread her folds and slide my tongue to her clit, where I flick and suck it before I thrust it inside her pussy. *God, she tastes so damn good.* I think to myself as I continue eating her.

"Oh, Oh...Declan," she calls out, and this spurs me on more.

"God, yes," she continues, as she writhes her body as I continue feasting on her pussy.

"FUCK," she screams out as she comes, her juices flooding my mouth, and I lap up every bit, causing her to have another orgasm, this one smaller than the first.

I kiss up her leg, then her stomach, stopping to lavish both her nipples as I swirl, flick, and suck each one. I kiss up her neck before finding her mouth. I kiss her deeply, both our tongues battling for more.

I position myself at her entrance and push in slowly, only pausing once the tip of my head is in. I slow our kiss down, wanting to take my time and enjoy the feeling of being with her. I push a little more, then slowly pull back, leaving the tip of my cock inside her, before pushing in further. I keep repeating this as I rotate my hips, soliciting moans from Kim.

"Declan, I need more," she breathes out.

"Soon. Right now, I want to enjoy how tight and wet you are. I need to take this slow," I tell her, rotating my hips and going deeper inside her.

I lean down and kiss her lips, intertwining our hands as I slowly thrust in and out of her.

"God, you feel so good," I whisper in her ear.

"Why did we wait so long?" she responds breathlessly with a moan while moving her hips to meet mine.

I can feel her walls starting to tighten, causing my spine to tingle. I pick up my pace, thrusting into her harder and faster.

"Oh God, Declan, yes," Kim calls out.

"Oh fuck," I breathe out, enjoying the feeling of her pussy wrapped around my cock as it tightens.

"I'm so close," she calls out.

I am too. I can feel my balls tightening up, but I need her to come first. I reach down in between us and roll her clit with my thumb, pressing down.

"Oh God, Oh God. YES, DECLAN," Kim screams out as the orgasm takes her over, and I follow suit, unloading my cum inside her.

"Kim," I grunt out as I come.

Once we both come down from our bliss, I kiss her lips before I slowly pull out of her. I catch her wince, and I say, "I'm sorry."

"Don't be, it's been a long while since I've done this," she tells me, and I'm actually stunned.

"How long?" I ask, curiosity getting the better of me.

"Years, and we will leave it at that, okay," she tells me, and I don't argue.

I roll to the other side of the bed, pulling her with me so that her head is on my chest.

"It's been years for me too," I whisper my honesty to her.

I can feel the small smile cross her face before she nestles into my chest to get comfortable. I know the minute she falls asleep because her breathing evens out and gets shallow. I close my eyes, happiness filling me, knowing that I finally have the woman that was made for me.

Chapter Five

KIM

I wake up with an arm wrapped around me, and it takes me a moment to remember what happened last night. I smile, thinking about the things Declan and I did, not just once, but several times last night. I would be content to just keep lying here, but my bladder is screaming.

I gently move Declan's arm and scoot out of the bed as quickly and quietly as possible, making my way to the bathroom. I quickly relieve myself, then flush the toilet. When I go to the sink to wash my hands, I look at myself in the mirror. My hair looks like I've been thoroughly fucked, which I had been. I can't help the smile that crosses my face as I remember how gentle and sweet Declan was the first time.

Of course, the second and third time were not as gentle or sweet, and I was more than okay with that. I quickly brush my teeth, then walk over to the shower to start the water. Once it's to the temp I want, I walk in and allow the hot water to cascade over me. I can feel the soreness between my legs. It's been a long time since I've had sex, much less three times in one night. I grab the loofa, slathering it with soap to wash myself.

I feel Declan walk into the bathroom before I see him. He climbs into the shower with me, wrapping his arms around me and grabbing the loofa from my hands.

"Let me," he whispers, and my legs turn to jelly.

He leans down and washes me, starting at the bottom of my left leg and slowly making his way up my thigh, only to switch to my right leg and stopping at my right thigh. He goes back to my left side, bringing the loofah to my inner thigh and moving so close to my pussy, but not touching it. He then goes and does the same thing on my right side, and again, not touching my pussy. He takes the loofah to my ass cheeks, doing one cheek at a time.

I can't help the moan that escapes me as he continues teasing and turning me on. He takes the loofa up my back, then down my arms one at a time, slowly. I want to groan as he continues to not touch me where I need him to.

"Are you okay?" he whispers with a chuckle, knowing exactly what he is doing since I am now rubbing my thighs together.

"No," I admit.

"Do you want me to stop?" he asks as he hovers the loofa over my stomach.

"No. I want more," I tell him as I lay the back of my head on his chest.

He chuckles and then begins to drag the loofah over my abdomen, up my sides, just grazing the outside of my breasts. My nipples tighten, needing his hands on me. I can feel his erection on my back, and I know I am not the only one affected by what he is doing. He takes the loofah up my neck, and then across the top of my chest, still not touching my breasts, when all of a sudden, the loofah is no longer in his hands, but his lips are on my neck, as one hand glides down to cup my pussy and the other one is squeezing my breast.

"God, yes," I moan out as he slides a finger inside me.

"Hmmm, so wet," he whispers in my ear before sucking on my earlobe.

He continues to finger me while I reach behind me, grabbing his cock, and pumping him.

He hisses in my ear, letting me know he is definitely okay with me touching him, too.

"Put your hands on the wall," he commands, and I can't help the gush of wetness that comes over him from his tone.

I do as he says, excited about what's to come.

He grabs my hips, pulling me back, then thrusts his cock deep inside me.

"Hmmm, your pussy is so greedy," he tells me as he thrusts in and out of me.

"Yes," I breathe out, enjoying the burn of the stretch and the pleasure of the friction that he is giving me.

"Damn, you feel so good," he moans as he continues to thrust into me while holding my hips with bruising authority.

I reach down and squeeze one of my breasts, pinching the nipple. "Yes, oh, God, yes," I call out as I feel my orgasm starting to build. I reach down between my legs and rub my clit, needing to come.

"That's it, baby, make yourself come all over my cock," he tells me, and I can't help but rub harder, wanting to do what he says.

"FUCK," I call out as I come hard.

"Yes, that's it," Declan says as he continues thrusting in me, getting deeper inside of me.

"Oh my God," I call out, feeling myself building again as he continues thrusting deep inside of me.

"God, yes. So....fucking....good," Declan says through gritted teeth.

I know he's holding off for me to have another orgasm, and before I can even think about it, I explode harder than I did before.

"MINE," Declan roars as he comes with me, and I feel him empty himself inside me.

It takes me a few minutes to come back into my body as I continue getting my breathing under control.

Declan kisses the side of my head, then says, "Good morning."

"Yes, that was definitely a good morning," I tell him, and he chuckles, pulling his softened cock out of me.

He turns me around and kisses my lips. When he pulls back, he tells me, "I meant what I said."

"What's that?" I ask, curious.

"You are mine. I'm not going anywhere, Kim. We will find a way to make this work, but I'm not going anywhere."

I can only stand there under the water of the shower, which has now turned cold, digesting his words. I only hope we can make this work. We both get out of the shower, me not responding to him since I'm not sure what to say.

Declan quickly dries off, puts the clothes that he wore last night back on, and leaves to go back to his place to get dressed and packed. We have an hour until we need to meet up with Heath and Frankie to go to the cabin for the weekend, so I quickly get dressed and pack an overnight bag.

I look over at my bed and see the evidence that last night was not a dream, nor was this morning in the shower, but I'm not sure how we are supposed to act this weekend in front of our co-workers. Especially since he just declared I was his, and he was not going anywhere. Can we keep this a secret? Should we keep this a secret? God, I'm so confused about what we should do.

I quickly strip the bed, get the bedding into the wash, and remake the bed with fresh sheets. Once I'm done, I look at the clock and know that it's time to leave. My heart is beating, happy to be spending time with Declan, but also nervous if we can keep our secret.

"I guess this will be our test," I say out loud as I grab my bag and walk out of my bedroom. When I get to the front door, I put my shoes on, grab my keys and purse, then open the door, "AHHH, EEEKKK," I scream, dropping my bag.

"Hey, it's okay," Declan says, putting his hands up.

"Damn it, you scared me again," I yell at him as I bend down to pick up my bag, but Declan does the same, and we bump heads.

"Oww," we both say at the same time as we rub our heads.

"I'm sorry," again at the same time.

This time, we both laugh at the silliness of everything.

"Are you okay?" Declan asks as he checks my head.

"Yeah, you?"

"I'll be fine," he tells me as he kisses the top of my head and then leans down and picks up my bag.

"What are you doing here?" I ask as I lock the front door.

"I thought we could spend our time riding together to the cabin. It's only an hour drive," he tells me as he puts my bag in the trunk of his car.

"That's nice, but what about Heath and Frankie? We are supposed to meet up with them and ride together," I remind him.

"I called Heath and told him you were having some car issues, and I would pick you up and drive you to the cabin," he informs me.

"And he believed you?" I ask incredulously. "No questions?"

"Of course, he questioned," Declan says with a sigh. "He wanted to know why you didn't call him?"

I laugh because that is exactly the question Heath would ask. "And?"

Declan sighs and says, "I told him that I was probably called because he knows nothing about vehicles like I do, and you didn't want the mechanics to take advantage of you."

"That's actually pretty good," I say, impressed.

"Yeah, he couldn't argue with that either, but he did say you needed to call him," he relays with another sigh while opening the passenger door for me.

"Thank you," I tell him as I lean up and give his lips a quick kiss before I get in the car.

He closes my door and then walks around the car to the driver's side.

Once he's in, he leans over, quickly takes my head, and slams his lips on mine, deepening the kiss. I immediately feel my body become needy as I tug on his hair while our tongues battle with each other.

I start to climb over the console, but Declan quickly breaks our kiss, both of us breathing hard.

"You need to sit back in your seat, dear, we have a cabin to get to," he says with a smirk on his face, but I know he was just as affected by that kiss as I was. I can see the outline of his hard bulge.

I pout, but he laughs. "I want you ready and needy for when we get home tomorrow evening," he tells me.

"That's not fair," I tell him as I rub my thighs together.

"No, but I want to be the one on your mind this weekend," he tells me.

"You have always been on my mind, and that will never change, especially now," I tell him honestly.

He leans over and kisses me quickly before he says, "Well, for that, I'll find us a place off the trail to get away to and ensure you come."

"Promise?" I breathe out.

"Well it will depend on how much time Heath wants from you and if I'm able to get you away," he tells me, sitting back in his seat and starting the car.

I laugh and say, "That's true."

We both buckle up and make the hour drive while talking about anything and everything.

When we get to the cabin, Heath is already there.

"Bestie, you didn't call me," he pouts as I get out of the car.

"Sorry hun. It's been a morning," I say exaggeratedly.

"Where's Frankie?" Declan asks.

"Oh, he called this morning and said he wasn't going to make it. Something about his dad wanting to see him," Heath tells us as we take our bags inside.

"I thought he said his dad was dead?" I question.

"Maybe he said he wished he was dead, cause I know he told me his relationship with his dad was non-existent, but maybe his dad is sick or something," Heath surmises, and I can only nod.

"Maybe I did hear him wrong," I say quietly, still trying to remember our exact conversation.

"Okay, let's go hit the trails," he adds.

"Wow, why are you so excited to hike?" I ask.

"I need some new profile pics," Heath says.

"Excuse me?"

"I need some new and updated pics for my dating profile. I need to show how active I am."

"Dating profile?" I ask.

"Yes, hunnybun. I told you about it when I asked if you wanted me to set up a profile for you since you need a man," he says, as though we really had this conversation.

"I don't recall this, but you know how I feel about online dating, also, I don't need a man," I say, feeling Declan watching me.

"It's not as bad as you think. I've had a couple of dates," he says, ignoring my comment about not needing a man.

"Then why are you wanting to update your photos?" I ask, curious.

"Because I need new blood, not duds," he says, grabbing his camera and handing it off to me.

"You want me to take pictures?" I ask, floored.

"Of course, you have an eye for things," he tells me with a smile as he ushers us out of the cabin and to the nearest hiking trail.

We hit the hiking trails and enjoy the fall colors of the trees as I take different photos of Heath as well as the environment.

The weekend turned out to be fun and relaxing, with lots of laughs.

Chapter Six

UNKNOWN

It's Saturday night, and I'm sitting in the shadows of the bar where I first saw her, watching as Marabel laughs with her friends. I haven't called her all week, wanting her to think I've moved on and she is safe. I can see how carefree she feels right now.

Her guard is down, and tonight is the night she will find out how I like to play my game. I have waited almost a month for this day, and I am beyond excited about what's to come. I continue nursing my beer while I wait and watch.

I watch as she decides to call it a night with her friends. While she says her good night, I leave the bar. I make it to her place, hiding in the shadows, listening for her to come down the sidewalk to her home.

I hear her talking on the phone in Spanish, though the conversation is one-sided since she wears earbuds, and I know immediately who she is talking to.

"No, mamá, estoy bien. Me voy a casa ahora mismo." *(No, mom, I'm good. I'm heading home right now.)*

"No, no más llamadas telefónicas, así que tal vez quienquiera que fuera se dio cuenta de que no valía la pena," *(No, no more phone calls, so maybe whoever it was realized I wasn't worth their time)* she tells her mom and I smile.

Soon, she'll know the truth.

"Por supuesto, vendré a cenar mañana, no me lo perdería," *(Of course, I'll be over for dinner tomorrow, I wouldn't miss it)* she says, and I can hear the smile in her voice.

There is no mistaking the love she has for her family.

"Sí, mamá, ya estoy en casa. Está bien, nos vemos mañana para cenar. Te amo, duerme bien," *(Yes, mama, I'm home now. Okay, I will see you tomorrow for dinner. Love you, sleep well)* she tells her mother before hanging up the phone as she walks up the steps to her front door.

I wait for her to open her front door, then I hit her upside her head knocking her out, catching her before she falls. I take her into her home, placing her on the stairs, as I grab her keys out of the door, pick up her purse, then close the front door. I place her purse and keys on the side table, take her earbuds out of her ears, and drop them in her purse.

I pull out the needle in my pocket and stick her in the arm, ensuring she doesn't wake up. I need to go get my car from across the street, but I don't want to risk her waking up.

I know I need to hurry since last call in the bars will be in an hour, and the streets will be filling with people walking home. Quickly and quietly, I walk out her front door, down the sidewalk, and across the street, where I left the car. I look around, seeing no one, I start the car up, leaving the lights off, and pull it around to the other side of the street. I leave it running with the lights off as I walk back up to her front door. I pick her up, close the front door, and carry her to the car, placing her in the back seat. I look around and make sure there are no witnesses while I climb in the driver's seat, pull away from the curb, and drive a little bit before I turn on the lights.

I continue driving, looking in the rearview mirror at my prey, still knocked out in the backseat. Giddiness hums through me, knowing I will soon get to play. I wonder how long she will last before she breaks.

Chapter Seven

KIM

Monday morning, I walk into the office after spending the weekend with Declan and Heath. Last night, after we got back home, Declan came and stayed the night with me, only leaving early this morning to go home and get ready for work.

Eric is already in his office, so I boot up my computer, wondering what today will have in store for us.

Mya walks in, making her way to her cubicle.

"Good morning," I say.

"Good morning," she responds.

"How was your weekend?" I ask her.

"It was good. How was the cabin and hiking?" she asks.

"It was fun, though it was only Declan, Heath, and I."

"Oh, what happened with Frankie?" she asks as he walks in.

"Good morning, Frankie, how was your visit with your dad?" I ask him.

"Huh? I didn't visit my dad," he says, confused.

"Oh? Heath said you couldn't make it this weekend because you had to go see your dad," I tell him, now very confused.

"No. I told him I had a last-minute date," Frankie says, shaking his head as he gets to his cubicle.

"Are you sure?" Heath asks, but no one notices when he walks in. "I'm pretty sure I know the difference between date and dad," he adds.

"I'm very sure," Frankie says.

"How did the date go?" I ask so as to keep them from arguing.

"It didn't. She stood me up," he admits, then adds, "So I spent the rest of the weekend in the gym, hitting the bag."

I look at his knuckles and see the bruises and cuts, letting me know he went hard on the bag.

"I'm sorry your weekend didn't go as planned, but you could have come to the cabin instead of hitting the gym," I tell him, sounding sympathetic.

He looks at me like I just offered to give him my kidney, and I realize I shouldn't have sounded so sympathetic.

I think he sees my discomfort because then he changes it up and says, "It was no big deal, plus I needed the workout. I'm sure you all had a good time regardless."

"Of course we had a good time," Heath says before adding, "Maybe you should get on a dating app," he tells him thoughtfully.

I roll my eyes before going back to my desk when Declan walks in. I can't help the smile that crosses my face, but I quickly school my features before I sit down and begin checking my emails.

Six months later

I leave Heath and Michelle at the park and make my way home from our run. Declan will be coming over tonight, and I want to get in the shower before he gets there. My phone rings, pulling me from my thoughts of Declan.

I hit the call button to activate my Bluetooth.

"Hello?" I answer

"Hello Kimberly," the distorted male voice says.

"Who is this?"

"Do you want a friend?"

"No, I have plenty," I tell the voice.

"I would love to be friends," he says before adding, **"Do you like games? I love games. Do you want to play a game?"**

"No, I don't, and don't call me again," I tell the voice before hanging up.

The phone rings again, and I answer, **"Hello?"**

"You shouldn't have hung up on me, Kimberly."

"Do you know who I am and what I do?" I ask.

"I know everything about you, Kimberly. We are going to become good friends," he tells me before hanging up this time.

"What the hell was that about?" I ask myself out loud.

I try to push the call from my mind, but I would be lying if I didn't admit that I'm a little bit creeped out by the fact that the caller seemed to know me.

"No, this must have been a prank call from someone I know," I try to convince myself. I mean, my personal number is private, there is no way someone who doesn't know me could get my number, so this must be a prank call.

I shake my head, believing it to be a prank and not dwelling on it, especially when I pull up to my house and see Declan is already here waiting on me.

I get out of the car and walk up the front walk to the house. The front door is unlocked, so I walk in. I place my purse and keys on the console table near the door, take off my running shoes, and walk into the house.

Finding Declan in the kitchen, I see he is wearing a pair of jeans and a light sweater. His blond hair is cut short, but not so short that I can't run my fingers through it. "Hey babe, you're early," I tell him, leaning up to kiss his lips.

"I hope you don't mind. I didn't want to wait until after you came back home," he tells me, wrapping his arms around me.

"Of course, I don't mind. If I did, I wouldn't have given you a key to my place," I tell him with a soft smile. I gave him a key to my place a couple of months ago as our relationship has progressed. "But right now, I need to go take a shower and change."

He leans down, kisses my lips, and says, "I would join you, but we would never get out of this house, and I have plans for tonight."

"Oh, I can't wait," I tell him as I laugh while walking to the bedroom.

Walking into the bathroom, I turn the shower on, strip out of my running clothes, and get in under the hot water. I quickly wash up, knowing Declan is waiting for me. I'm excited to see what surprise he has in store for us tonight.

I get out of the shower, dry off, and walk into my closet. I quickly pick out a pair of jeans and a long-sleeve shirt. It may be spring, but the nights are still cool. I pull everything on and add a pair of calf-high boots before walking back into my bathroom to brush out my hair.

I don't bother to blow dry my hair, as it will just frizz up, so I allow it to air dry. I walk back to the living room to find Declan sitting on the couch. As soon as he sees me, he jumps up and says, "Wow, you look absolutely stunning."

I can't help the blush that creeps up my neck and face. Some days, I'm still in awe that we are here together. It's been six months, and still, we've managed to keep our secret, though Frankie makes it hard with his constant barrage of pleas to go on a date.

I know there are going to be issues when Declan and I finally come out, and I shudder to think what is going to happen. I know Declan wants to make our relationship known, he's hinted at it several times, more so because of Frankie.

Almost as if Declan can read my mind, "Maybe we should talk before we go to dinner," he says.

I sigh. I had hoped that we could hold off for a little while longer. "Can we focus on us tonight, please? I know we need to discuss how to move forward, but I only want tonight to be about us and reaching a milestone in our relationship," I tell him.

Today is our six-month anniversary, and I just want to enjoy it without the pressures of anything else.

He looks at me, almost as if he wants to argue, but then concedes. "Okay, tonight can be about us, but tomorrow, we need to talk."

I nod and give him a huge smile.

He shakes his head, then pulls me in for a hug while kissing the top of my head, before leading me to the front door.

"Where are we going?" I ask him as I grab my purse while he slips his shoes on.

"Where we started," he says with a laugh as I look at him.

"We are going to DC?" I ask, confused.

"Not that far back," he tells me, shaking his head while he laughs.

We get in the car and he drives us to the Mexican restaurant, I can't help the blush that takes over me as the memories of our first time together rush through me. It was right after we left the restaurant.

Declan parks the car, then comes around to open my door and helps me out. We walk hand in hand into the restaurant and are greeted by the hostess.

"Good evening, two?" she asks, giving us a knowing smile.

"Yes, please," Declan and I both say at the same time.

She leads us to the same corner table we were at on our first date. I can't help but smile at the memories.

We both order our water with lemon, as well as the Queso Fundito, before perusing the menu.

I decide I'm going to order the same thing I had that night, six months ago.

The waitress comes back with our waters and Queso Fundito, and I order the enchiladas with chicken, but this time, I don't get the meal. I remember how big everything was, and it was too much for me to eat.

Declan orders his Puffy Tacos as a meal. Where the man puts everything, I have no clue, as his body, even at forty-one, looks like a muscled God.

"I don't want to talk about work, but what do you think of this new serial killer case we may have?" Declan asks quietly.

Michelle informed Eric and I that there may be a serial rapist/killer, but she hasn't figured out how he's killing his victims. They are found in lakes, but there is no water in their lungs to suggest drowning. He seems to suffocate his victims, but she can't figure out how.

"I'm not sure. There are so many questions and not enough answers. All the scenes are similar, how does he find them? Does he stalk his victims, or are they victims of opportunity? I'm sure once we figure out who, the why may make sense, but it's finding the who before there is another victim."

"How is Michelle doing?" he asks.

"Not great. You know, she takes these victims personally, especially if she thinks she missed something that could have saved another victim," I tell him with a sigh.

"Okay, enough about work. This is our sixth month together, and I want us to celebrate being together, but I'm not going to lie, Kim, I want to tell the team sooner rather than later. I'm at the point with Frankie that I want to knock him out every time he alludes to being in love with you."

I spit out my drink. "What? I mean, I know he wants to be more than friends, but love?" I choke out.

Declan looks hurt when he says, "Yeah. When he and I are together, that's all he talks about. He thinks you'll learn to love him too."

I see the pain in his eyes, and I'm not sure what to do or say. I don't want to hurt Declan, but the only way Frankie can't cause problems for us is if we are honest with the team and one of us gets a reassignment somewhere else. To be honest, I don't know that our relationship could survive the separation.

We both get quiet as we ponder over this dilemma. The waitress brings our food over, placing each plate in front of us. Looking at it, I no longer have an appetite. I know Declan is hurt, and it's the last thing I want to do, but I don't see a way out of this. I need to talk to my best friend, but I also need to be careful with how much I tell her.

Though nothing has been said, I'm pretty sure she and Eric are dating, though I don't know how they find time. If she's not working at the morgue, she's lecturing at conferences, but the marks both Heath and I saw on her, there is no mistaking she is seeing someone. I'm just a little hurt that she has not told me about them.

Right now, Declan and I have no choice but to continue keeping our relationship a secret, at least until we figure out everything else. So much for having a wonderful six-month anniversary date.

Chapter Eight

DECLAN

I should have kept my feelings to myself, especially tonight. I hate keeping us a secret, but I would hate to lose Kim even more.

"Hey, let's not think about anything but us tonight. This is our night, and I don't want to ruin it. I'm sorry I said anything," I tell her, reaching over and taking her hand in mine, where it belongs. "How about we finish this lovely meal, no more talk about work, and then when we get home, I can show you exactly how special you are to me," I tell her, smiling as I recall my special surprise for her.

I watch her eyes light up at the word show, and I know immediately where her mind goes. I can't help the laugh that escapes me. "You have such a dirty mind," I tell her.

"I can't help it, you have a way of bringing that side out of me," she says seductively, and my cock thickens in my pants.

"So, if I told you I have a special surprise for you?"

"Is it of the gift nature or dirty nature?" she asks.

I pretend to ponder her question before I say, "There could be some ice, some chocolate, lots of tasting, licking, sucking," I say, lowering my voice with each word until I say the last one in a whisper, "and when we are done with that, then a whole lot of fucking."

"Check please," she calls out breathlessly.

"Are you sure you are done eating?" I ask her as I rub the inside of her wrist, feeling her pulse throb.

"I'm sure," she says as the waitress comes to the table.

"Would you like a couple of boxes for your food?" she asks, leaving the check on the table.

"No, I don't think we will need them this time," I tell her, handing her the cash to cover the bill and tip.

She smiles knowingly, "Have a good night," she chuckles while clearing the table, and we head for the door.

I get Kim settled in the car, and I walk around to the driver's side. My cock is hard with the anticipation of what is to come for the night.

We get back to Kim's place, and as soon as we walk into the house, I pull her into me, kissing her lips. Our kiss turns from sweet and soft to frenzy within seconds. I lift her up, and she immediately wraps her legs around me.

I carry her to the bedroom, laying her on the bed. I pull her pants off her slowly, wanting to prolong this adventure as much as I can.

"Declan, please," she calls out, but I won't be rushed.

I kiss up her stomach slowly, as I push up her shirt over her bra. I kiss the tops of her breasts, pushing her shirt up her arms and kissing her neck. I get the shirt over her head, throwing it to the floor.

I straddle her legs, ensuring I keep my weight off her, as I take in her perfectly tanned body. She still has her underwear and bra on, covering her most intimate parts.

"You are so gorgeous," I tell her.

"And you have too many clothes on," she quips back.

"I'm not done yet," I say as I smirk at her. I reach over into the nightstand.

"What are you...?" she starts to ask until she sees the handcuffs. "Ohhh..."

"Do you trust me, Kim?" I ask her.

I watch as she gulps, taking in not only the handcuffs but the blindfold I am holding up. I watch as her tongue darts out and licks her lips while chill bumps coat her skin and her nipples harden under her bra.

"Yes, I trust you," she replies breathlessly.

"Good girl," I tell her as I lift her arms above her head and handcuff her to the wooden headboard. I slip the blindfold over her eyes, then kiss her lips, and then say softly, "I want you to feel everything I do to you tonight."

She takes a sharp breath, and I can't help but admire her beauty. I kiss the tops of her breasts and listen to her breathing change to a slow moan.

I get up off her and the bed. "I'll be right back," I tell her, leaving the room.

"What? Where are you going?" she calls out.

I shake my head as I make my way to the kitchen to get my surprise. The true reason why I was here early.

"Declan, you better not have done this to leave me like this," she yells out.

I walk back in and say, "I thought you trusted me?"

I place the goodies on the nightstand and strip out my clothes.

"I do, but you never know what someone is thinking when they handcuff you to the bed and blindfold you, then they say I'll be back," she tells me, sounding frustrated.

I climb back on the bed, kissing her neck, and then I whisper in her ear, "I would never allow someone else to find you looking so delectable."

She takes in a sharp breath as I touch her softly. I undo her bra, lifting it up her arms before I latch my mouth on her nipple, sucking hard.

"Oh, Declan," she moans out while my tongue flicks her nipple as it hardens under my tongue.

I switch my mouth to the other, doing the same. I lean up, skimming my hands down her sides, then grab her panties, pulling them down her legs.

Her pussy is glistening, and I smile, knowing she wants me.

I reach over to the nightstand, grabbing my first surprise, chocolate syrup. I swirl some over her nipples.

"What is that?" she asks curiously.

I don't say anything as I take my finger and rub it around her areolas, then I latch my mouth over one, sucking and licking.

This causes her to moan. Her body is so receptive that I can't help the moan that escapes me as I continue to suck and lick.

I blow on her nipples as I pick the chocolate back up and drizzle it down her tight stomach before licking and sucking every bit of it, as I make my way to heaven.

I drizzle some chocolate on her pelvic bones, kissing and sucking, causing her to buck and writhe, but I hold her down, and she starts to beg.

"Declan, please. I can't take anymore, I need you."

I chuckle. "Oh, sweetheart, I haven't even started yet," I whisper to her as I get back to licking and sucking the chocolate on her body.

I work my way down to the top of her shaven pussy. I kiss the top of it, before leaning up to grab my next surprise off the nightstand. I place the ice cube and move over her clit.

"Oh my God, that's cold. What the hell is that?" she calls out.

I move the ice cube and replace my mouth over her clit, as I suck and flick it with my tongue.

"OH MY GOD," she screams out as I continue sucking her clit, while my finger enters her pussy, I finger her sweet spot.

I pull my finger from her wet pussy, place the ice cube back in my mouth, and thrust my tongue inside her pussy, slurping up her juices while using my tongue to thrust the ice cube inside her.

"OH, FUCK!" she screams out, trying to buck up as I hold her down at her abdomen while fucking her with my tongue and the ice cube until the ice cube melts.

"OH, FUCK," she continues to call out as I continue eating her out.

I feel her legs quiver, her walls tighten, and I know her orgasm is close. I pick up the pace of my tongue as I shove my face into her pussy, when her juices flood my mouth as she comes.

"OH FUCK, DECLAN!" she screams out.

I lap up all her juices. My cock is so hard that I can't wait any longer. I line my cock at her entrance and thrust hard and deep.

"OH MY GOD," she calls out.

I reach up, pull the blindfold off her, and uncuff her hands. I want to feel her hands on me.

"You feel so fucking good, Kim. Hot, wet, and needy. I love how responsive your body is," I tell her as I thrust deeper.

"So good," she says breathlessly, while matching my thrusts with her own.

Her nails rake down my back, and I can't help but enjoy the pain as it spurs me on.

"Declan, I need more," she tells me.

I put her legs over my shoulders and thrust into her, going deeper than before.

"OH, FUCK, YES!" she screams out, and I can't help but to thrust harder and faster.

"Fuck, baby, you are so tight," I tell her.

"Oh, don't stop. Please don't stop, Declan. You feel so good," she tells me.

"Never," I grunt out as I thrust harder and deeper.

The slapping of our slick skins and moans is the only thing you can hear in the room right now. Kim rakes her nails down my arms as I feel her walls tighten again, this time strangling my cock.

"Oh, God," I moan. "Fuck, you're killing me," I grit out through my teeth, trying so hard not to come prematurely.

I move her legs off my shoulders, and she immediately wraps them around my waist as we both meet each other's thrusts. I lean down and kiss her lips, feeling her breasts rub up and down my chest, both of us slick with sweat.

"Fuck, babe, I'm going to come soon," I tell her as I feel my balls tightening up.

"I'm so close," she says with a moan.

I thrust deeper, picking up the pace, needing her to come before I do, but my cock starts to swell, and I come hard inside her, causing her to come at the same time.

"OH KIM," I call out.

"DECLAN!" she screams at the same time.

I continue thrusting as I unload inside her until there is nothing left. Both of us are breathing hard as we come down from our orgasmic bliss.

I pull my softened cock out of her and roll onto the bed next to her, trying to catch my breath.

"That was amazing," she says, breathless.

"Yes, it was," I respond.

"What did you use on me?" she asks.

"Chocolate syrup and ice cube. Did you like it?" I ask sheepishly.

"No, I didn't like it. I loved it. That was an experience I wouldn't mind trying again," she tells me with a smile.

I smile back at her, happy to know I gave her a wonderful surprise.

"Come on woman, let's get a shower, clean you up, and then get some sleep," I tell her, getting up from the bed and giving her my hand to help her up.

"Sounds good," she says, with a smile on her face.

We get in the shower, and I wash her up before tucking her into bed in my arms for the night.

Chapter Nine

UNKNOWN

Marabel was fun for a while. Her fear made me giddy. I had so much fun breaking her, and I have enjoyed my time with her, but I'm becoming bored again. I needed a new challenge, and I found her.

Kimberly Santiago. She won't break so easily, and I'm looking forward to the challenge. I am already imagining all the fun we will have.

She thinks I don't know who she is, but I do. Her FBI status isn't going to stop me. I'm smarter than the FBI.

They don't even realize they have more than one serial killer so close to them. They are currently chasing a serial rapist/killer, but he leaves his bodies in plain sight to be found. I would never be so foolish.

I've been hiding bodies for years. Some have been found, and others have not, but no one has put together that there is one killer.

People go missing, you hear it on the news all the time. Some parent, spouse, or family member gets on TV requesting help in finding their loved one.

Marabel's parents were on the TV, looking for help, even offering a reward, but unfortunately, they may never find her, well at least not right away.

I laugh, unable to help myself as I make my way to purchase more burner phones, one's that can't be traced back to a store, at least not by me anyway.

I know how the FBI will operate. They are not much different from the local law enforcement when they are dealing with a case. They will check phone records, they will check their case files, and they will scratch their heads as they try to figure out what happened.

All the while, I will have their agent that they will never see again. I can't help the laugh that escapes me again as I see images of how things will play out.

Soon, I will make my move, but first, I have much to prepare.

Chapter Ten

KIM

One month later

The last month has been a whirlwind. First, I find out my best friend married my boss in secret, then taken by our serial killer, who turned out to be a priest.

Declan and I have decided to keep our relationship a secret from the team for a while longer, especially after he found out that Eric and Michelle are actually married, and none of us even knew.

I think back on the conversation we had leading up to the decision.

"What do you mean you're thinking about transferring back to the DC field office?"

"Declan, neither of us want to keep our relationship a secret anymore, but the only way we are going to be honest with everyone is if one of us transfers. I would never ask you to leave this team."

"So, you think it's okay if you leave?"

"I don't see any other way," I tell him, tears brimming in my eyes.

He rubs the back of his head as he paces the room. I know he is struggling with the situation just as much as I am.

He turns and looks at me. "Kim, listen to me. If you were to transfer, neither one of us would be happy not seeing the other. We would both be miserable and unable to do our jobs."

"I know you are right, but what else can we do?" I ask him.

"Does it suck? Yes. Would I prefer to be honest with everyone? Absolutely."

"Me too," I whisper.

He grabs my hands and says, "I know you do, but as a team, we made a rule, and as long as Frankie thinks he has feelings for you..." *he starts to say, and I cut in.*

"We both know he doesn't really feel anything for me except infatuation. The man doesn't even know me beyond my work ethic."

"I know, babe, but in his mind, he thinks he is in love with you. If he should ever find out about us, you know as well as I do, he will cause havoc in the team," *Declan says, with sadness in his eyes.*

"That's why I think it would be better if I leave the team. We will no longer have to hide our relationship, and maybe if I'm no longer on the team, he will get over his infatuation with me," *I tell him softly.*

"Babe, he will just blame me for you leaving, and there will still be strife in the team. Frankie is still mentally young. Nothing we say or do is going to make anything better."

"What are you trying to say, Declan?"

"I'm saying if Michelle and Eric could keep their relationship a secret and then their marriage, I see no reason why we can't either. We've made it over six months already, what's a little more time?" he says, trying to muster a small smile.

"But I know that's not what you really want, hell that's not what I want..." I start to say.

"It may not be what I or we want, but for the moment, it's our only option. I cannot live in a place without you. I love you, Kim, you are it for me, and if it means keeping what we have between us as secret, then I am willing to do just that," he tells me, and I can see the truth of his words shining back at me through his eyes.

"I love you too, Declan," I whisper, tears in my eyes as I admit how I've been feeling all these years. "I have always loved you."

He gives me a big smile, "And I have always loved you. We will get through this, but for now, we just keep doing what we have been. You did say Michelle told you secret relationships had their perks," he gives me a seductive grin.

"She did say that," I say with my own grin as he leans down and kisses me.

Shelly, Heath, Frankie, and I meet up with Chris at the park for our weekly run. Declan opted not to come with us today, letting me know there was something he needed to take care of, but wouldn't tell me what when I asked.

I look over at Shelly as we stretch, and she seems to be doing better since her kidnapping from the serial killer.

I will never forget the terror and panic that clawed at me when I didn't see my best friend here for our run. After running all over the park, I realized that the serial killer had her. When we finally found her and I saw the priest on top of her, I was stunned.

I was happy that we saved her and grateful to have found the killer, but I know she's had a hard time dealing with the aftermath. Today, she looks better, smiling and laughing, letting me know she is on the mend.

"Chris, I never asked, but what do you do?" Shelly asks.

"I'm a software engineer," he says, shrugging his shoulders.

"That is amazing," she responds with a smile.

"Do you even know what that means, Shell?" Heath asks with a grin.

She stands up, puts her hands on her hips, and says, "It means he works in the IT Department somewhere and handles all the software that gets loaded."

Chris chuckles, "Yes, for the most part, though there is more to it."

"I'm sure there is," she responds with a smile to Chris before giving Heath a glare.

"Wow, sugar britches, I was just asking," Heath says, throwing his hands up in defeat.

"Are we going to run or talk?" Frankie asks, sounding bored and looking tense.

"Why? Do you have a hot date tonight?" Heath asks.

"Maybe," Frankie responds, looking over at me but offering nothing else.

Heath looks over at me, and I can only shrug and shake my head.

"Let's go," Shelly says.

She and I take the lead on the trail as we talk about some of the wedding details.

We have two months until Shelly and Eric's second wedding at a cabin that Eric bought for her as a wedding gift in Cedar. Shelly took me over there, and it's absolutely gorgeous and is the perfect place to have a summer wedding. The lake is calming, beautiful, and majestic. It will make the perfect backdrop as they say their vows.

Shelly and I are in complete planning mode. We decided to have the food catered and have chosen a local restaurant in Cedar.

"We still need to find a DJ, make a makeshift dance floor, get tents and chairs," Shelly says.

"Yeah, there is still so much to do," I tell her, "But we have plenty of time. I'll look into local DJs and see if I can set up some interviews," I add.

"That would be great. I have a conference coming up, and I feel like I'm putting everything on you," she says with a sigh.

"It's fine, this is what best friends and maid-of- honors are for," I say, trying to soothe her nerves.

"I feel so guilty. This is my wedding, and I'm barely able to do anything," she whines a little.

"You are helping where it is needed. You decided on the place and gave me your plans on how you wanted it to look. We have chosen a very nice restaurant to cater, and you decided on the menu. I will record the DJs and allow you to choose which one you want to hire. As for the tents, tables, and chairs, I can handle the logistics. However, you will need to make time to go by the floral shop and decide on your flowers," I tell her.

"Noted," she says with a smile before adding, "I'm so glad I have you, otherwise, I don't think any of this would be happening."

"True. You would have had to deal with knowing your only wedding took place in Vegas," I tell her with a smirk.

"Hey, it was a very nice little chapel," she says with a smirk of her own.

"Others won't know that. They hear Vegas and think of a chapel on the strip with Elvis," I say, laughing out loud, and she joins in.

"What's so funny up there?" Heath calls out.

"Vegas," we both say simultaneously, then bust out laughing even more.

"You're having wedding conversations without me?" Heath asks, and I can hear the sadness in his voice.

"I didn't think you wanted to be involved in all the planning details," Shelly says, looking back at him.

"Who said that?" he asks.

"You," we both say.

"Huh?" he asks, looking utterly confused.

"Don't you remember saying, 'I'm not a wedding planner, manual labor is not my thing. The only thing I want to be in charge of is wardrobe,' and when we told you we already had our dresses, you pouted," Shelly tells him.

"Well, it's true, fashion is my thing, so I want to see these dresses before the big day. Especially yours, Kimmy," he says, not commenting on the manual labor part at all.

"Why especially mine?"

"You have no fashion sense, and I refuse to allow you to embarrass our lady of honor," he states.

Shelly and I both bust out laughing, "Lady of honor?" we question at the same time.

"She is the mistress of the day, and since you will be standing up next to her, I refuse to allow you to look like a hot mess," he says dramatically.

"I would never," I say, actually offended.

"Not on purpose," he says with a shrug.

I can't help but huff at his insinuation that I have no style.

"Don't worry about it. I'm sure your dress is beautiful, and you will look amazing no matter what," Shelly whispers to me, but now I'm worried it won't be.

We get done with our run, and Heath leaves with Chris. I wave goodbye to everyone as I pull out of the parking lot.

I'm mentally making a list of things I need to do for the wedding when my phone rings. I completely forget to look at the caller ID and instead answer the call.

"Hello?"

"Kim...ber...ly," the voice on the phone sings out. **"Are you ready to play my game?"**

I shudder at the voice. For the last few months, my phone has constantly rang with the restricted number, and I've been good about not answering it, until now.

I shake my head, **"No, and quit calling me before I have you arrested for stalking,"** I tell him before I hang up.

The phone rings again, and I ignore it until the third time it rings, then I answer, **"What do you want?"**

"Whoo, are you okay?" I hear Declan ask.

"Sorry. I've been bombarded with telemarketer calls recently, and it's just getting annoying," I tell him with frustration in my voice.

"I'm sorry. I was just calling to see if you wanted to meet up for dinner?"

"I would love to, but I also have a lot of wedding things I need to jot down and research for," I say with another heavy sigh.

"How about we do it together? I'll come pick you up, we can grab a bite and go over notes."

"That sounds good," I agree, feeling a bit of the weight come off my shoulders.

"Okay, I'll see you in a few minutes, love you," he tells me.

"Love you too," I say, with a smile on my face.

I pull into the driveway, lock my car, and walk toward the front door. I stick the key in the lock, and with my mind on Declan, I never heard him come up behind me. I feel the pain to my head, then everything goes black.

Chapter Eleven

DECLAN

Present Day

It's been almost a month since Kim disappeared. That night replays over in my head.

I had just talked to her and planned on taking her out to dinner. There was something I wanted to ask her now that the serial killer case had been solved. I couldn't have been more than five minutes behind her since we hung up, but when I got to her house, I found the door unlocked, her purse on the console table next to the door with her keys next to it.

I walk to the bedroom, wondering if she quickly jumped in the shower, knowing I wasn't far behind, but she's not in the room. I can tell imme-

diately that she never came into the bathroom to shower. I pull my phone out and call her, but it goes straight to voicemail.

"That's not like her to turn her phone off," I say out loud.

I try the track location, however, there is nothing. I get an uneasy feeling, but instead of jumping to conclusions, I call Michelle.

"Declan, what's going on?"

"Hey, Michelle, is Kim with you? Did you have plans tonight?"

"No, she's not with me, and we don't have plans to meet tonight."

My heart sinks.

"She's gone," I tell her, trying to keep the panic I'm feeling out of my voice.

"What do you mean she's gone?"

"Her car is here at the house, but she is not. I called her phone, and it went straight to voicemail. We were supposed to have dinner tonight, and she knew I was going to pick her up," I explain to her, allowing some of the fear I feel to convey in my voice.

"So why did you think she would be with me?" she asks me, sounding worried.

"I just hoped maybe she got tied up with you on some wedding things, but you say no, and I don't know where else she could be, I'm concerned," I tell her.

Then Eric chimes in, "Declan, you said her car is there?"

"Yes, Boss. It's parked in the driveway and locked."

"Did you go inside and see if anything is out of place?"

"Yes, Boss. Her keys are on the table by the door, with her purse, but I don't see her phone, and nothing else looks to be disturbed," I tell him.

"Did you try to track her phone?"

"Yes, sir, and it's not registering, telling me it's off," I inform him.

"Let me call Frankie and Heath and see if she said anything to them before she left the park," Michelle says before hanging up.

When the phone rings, I ask, "Do they know anything?"

"Did you check the grocery store down from her house to ensure she didn't walk down there?" she immediately asks.

"No, but I'll head that way now," I tell her.

"Call me back," she says before hanging up.

I run down to the grocery store that I know she frequents. She was not there, and when I asked the cashiers and employees, no one had seen her today.

I run around to the other stores in the area just in case, but she's not there, and no one has seen her.

My heart is beating wildly, and I have a sinking feeling. "Something's happened to her," I whisper to myself as I call Michelle back.

"She's not at the grocery store, or at any of the shops. No one has seen her today," I tell her as panic begins to set inside me.

"Call the team and tell them to meet at the office. One of our own is missing, and we need to find out why," Eric says through the phone.

My hands are shaking as I call Mya first, "Declan, what's going on?",

"Eric wants everyone at the office, Kim is missing," I tell her and immediately hung up and do the same for Heath and Frankie.

I know they all wanted to know more, but I had nothing more to give them.

"Where are you, Kim?" I say out loud.

We meet in the conference room, and once Eric tells the group what we know so far, Mya immediately suggests she contact taxi companies and request Uber and Lyft's data, airports, and the train station to see if she left in a hurry somewhere. Michelle went to call Kim's mom, while Heath and I were tasked to go back through her house to see if we missed anything and talk with her neighbors. Frankie was tasked with her phone log for the last three months.

Every day, we worked different angles, looking through old cases for anyone who may have wanted to harm her.

Mya and Heath got called away to a serial killer in Boston, so it was just Eric, Frankie, and I trying to find answers about where Kim could be. Every night, I have been on the streets, looking for information, anything to find Kim. Sleeping very little, needing to find her.

I've been slowly going out of my mind for the last month, staying at her place, looking for clues. I've scoured the city nightly, only eating when I was forced to, like the night Mya and Heath came in from Boston, and Mya suggested we all eat together. They brought Detective Shane Mcguire back with them to get some footage from our train station.

I had suggested the Italian place down the road, and the meal was good as was the company, but inside, I felt guilty for taking time away from looking for Kim, but Mya was right, we needed to clear our heads and look at things from another perspective. That was the first night that I actually went back to Kim's place and slept.

I was on the streets again, when Eric called me to come to the hospital. I thought something happened to Michelle, especially since when I asked, all he told me was he would tell me when I got here.

My mind is racing as I walk into the emergency room, looking around until I see Eric, and then I see Michelle next to him. She looks good, nothing I can see outwardly to warrant an emergency room visit. My shoulders deflate with the tension I had been holding, but now, I'm curious as to why he called me here.

Of all the things he could have said, I was not expecting Eric's next words that Kim was here in the hospital, and we had to wait for the doctor.

Now I'm sitting here next to her bed, listening to the machines whirl and beep, the only sound in the quiet hospital room. I stare at the woman who stole my heart so many years ago, still unable to comprehend that after almost a month, she is here.

Currently, she's lying so still in the hospital bed with IV lines placed in her arm. She has a blood pressure cuff around her upper arm and a pulse reader on her finger.

I take in the bruises, the cast, and can see some of the wire in her mouth where the doctor said they had to wire it shut to fix it.

Seeing her like this, I can't help the guilt I feel for not doing more. Someone hurt the woman I love more than anything in this world. I need to find them and make them pay for what they did to her.

The problem is I don't know everything they did. How will she be when she wakes up? What if she hates me for not saving her? I mean, the woman saved herself, finding her way to the morgue.

My mind is whirling with every negative thought that my mind can conjure up, but I squeeze her hand, reminding myself she is here and I will do everything to protect her from here on out.

"I'm so glad you found your way back to us, Kim. I've been looking everywhere, trying to find you, and so has the team. We scoured through every case file during the day, and at night, I've been working every contact on the streets," I whisper to her as I continue sitting next to her bed, holding her hand that is not in a cast, as tears glisten in my eyes.

"I promise I will protect you, and whoever did this, we will catch them, and I will make them pay for all the pain they caused you," I vow to her.

The door opens and I quickly jump up from my seat, whirling around to see who is entering.

"It's just me, Agent. I've come to check on Agent Santiago's vitals," the nurse who brought us up here tells me.

I nod to her as I walk over to the wall between the door and Kim's bed. I watch the nurse as she adjusts Kim's lines and jots down notes on Kim's chart.

When she's done, she gives me a weak smile before asking, "Would you like me to have a cot brought in so you can get some sleep?"

"No, thank you," I tell her softly.

There is no way I can sleep right now as long as Kim is lying so still in that bed, unable to defend herself.

She nods in understanding, "There will be nurses coming in and out of the room throughout the night and early morning hours," she tells me, and it's my turn to nod in understanding.

She leaves the room, closing the door behind her. I go back to the seat that I vacated when she walked in, wrapping my hand around Kim's, and sit here staring at her.

True to her word, nurses come in throughout the night, taking notes of her vitals and changing her bags of IV. Each time I'm asked about a cot, and I can only shake my head no. At one point during the night, the original nurse who came in brought me some coffee when she came in to check on Kim.

"Here, I figured you could probably use this," she tells me with a smile, handing me the cup.

"Thank you," I say softly.

I sip the hot coffee, grateful for the heat and caffeine. I walk over to the window, looking out, and I can see the sun starting to peek through the night. The sky has a hue of orange, and I know it won't be long before the sun rises, indicating the start of a new day.

The nurse leaves Kim and I alone again, and I stare at her while I continue sipping on the coffee as I take a seat in the chair I vacated.

The next time the door opens, Michelle and Eric are walking in. I look at my watch and see it's eight in the morning already.

"Any changes?" Michelle asks.

"No. Aside from the nurses coming in and out of the room, it's been a quiet night," I say as I stand and throw my empty coffee cup away.

I'm pretty sure Michelle knows about Kim and I, I don't know if Eric is fully aware of our relationship, but I watch his head nod, taking in what I said.

"Have you gotten any sleep?" he asks.

"No, Boss."

"Go home," he starts to say.

"Boss, I can't...someone needs..." I interrupt him, but he shuts me down and takes back the conversation.

"Yes, you can. You need to sleep. You look like shit. Michelle will stay with Kim this morning, and Kim will never be alone. I plan to tell the team she has been found once I get to the office. We will set up a schedule for everyone to take shifts watching over Kim, but if you want to be on that schedule, you need to sleep," he tells me sternly.

"Don't worry, Declan, I promise I will not leave her," Michelle tells me softly as she lays her hand on my arm.

I look over at Kim, still lying on the bed, unmoving. Wavering with what I should do and what I am being told to do. I promised Kim I would protect her. If I leave her, then I can't protect her.

"Declan," Eric says my name with authority in his voice.

"Boss, I promised her last night I would protect her. I can't do that if I'm not here," I tell him honestly, as my voice cracks.

"Declan, she will be protected, but you cannot protect her if you fall out from exhaustion. You will only be letting her down when she needs you the most," Michelle tells me softly, showing me she understands how I feel.

I know she's right, I know they both are, but I'm having a hard time walking out of this hospital room, knowing we have her back right now, but what happens if I leave and realize this was all a dream?

"I promise, Declan, I will not leave her until you get back. We need you to rest. She needs you to be at a hundred percent. If you love her, like I think you do, then you need to take care of yourself so you can take care of her," Michelle tells me.

I look over at Kim and whisper, "I do love her. I always have," I admit.

"I know," Michelle says, and I look back at her. She has tears in her eyes, "I promise Declan, I won't leave her."

"You need to go home and get some sleep, Declan," Eric says softly. "I'll even drive you to make sure you get there safely," he adds, going back into boss mode.

"Okay, but you promise you won't leave her?' I ask Michelle.

"I promise," she tells me.

I look back over at Kim, still lying in the bed, the machines still beeping. I look back at Eric and nod, knowing they are right, and I have no choice.

I allow Eric to lead me out of the hospital and into his car.

"Does Kim know how you feel?" Eric asks.

"Yes, Boss, she does."

"How long have you two been in a relationship?"

"Six months, but please don't tell the team," I ask him.

"Why? They had no issues with Michelle and I being together when we told them."

"It's Frankie. He thinks he's in love with Kim, and one day she will love him too. He has these dreams of them together," I tell him, shaking my head.

"Ahh, and with the internal no dating rule you all set, you think there could be an issue," he says, understanding.

"Yes, Boss. He will definitely cause chaos in and for the team," I say with a sigh.

"I'll keep it quiet until you all are ready, and then we will deal with everything as a team."

"Thanks, Boss. Also, I want to be the only one on the nightshift protecting Kim. It's not that I don't trust the team..." I say, allowing the words to fall off.

"I get it. I would be the same if the roles were reversed, and it was Michelle."

I look over at him and see he really does understand. I feel better knowing I will be with Kim every night.

I pull my phone out and set my alarm for five pm, just in case I forget to do it when I get home.

Eric drops me off at my apartment, which is closer to the hospital than Kim's is. He waits for me to go in, and once I close the door, the exhaustion I've kept at bay finally takes hold of my body, and I barely muster the energy to make it to the bedroom before I collapse on the bed.

Chapter Twelve

ERIC

After leaving Declan at his place, I drive over to the office, knowing the team is waiting and probably wondering where I am.

I walk into the office and see Mya smiling and Frankie stewing in his cubicle, looking at his phone.

"Mya, where's Heath?" I ask her.

She and Heath just got back yesterday from Boston after solving the Train Murders and bringing Rayeanne back home to her family.

"He's gone to see his primary care physician for his concussion as you instructed him yesterday," she tells me, looking at me with knowing eyes.

"What's wrong? Is Michelle okay?" she asks, then looks around, "Where's Declan?" Weariness is in her voice as the smile she just had disappears.

I look at both of my agents knowing I need to wait for Heath.

"When Heath gets in, we will talk," I tell them as I walk to my office.

I take a deep breath as I place my face in my hands. I didn't get much sleep last night, as questions about Kim kept popping up.

Where has she been? Who took her? Why did they beat her like that? What else did they do? Will she be okay mentally, and how will that affect her relationship with the team?

I try to focus on the emails in my inbox, but I can't. Memories of Kim collapsing in the doorway of Michelle's office, her battered and bloody body assail me. Seeing her hooked up to the machines at the hospital has my head reeling.

This is my team. I meant to keep them safe, and I failed. I failed my wife's best friend. I chastise myself internally when there is a knock at the door.

I look up and see Heath standing there. My body deflates, knowing I have no choice now but to tell the team.

"Boss, you wanted to know when I returned?"

"Yeah, did the doctor give you clearance to work?" I ask him.

"Light duty for three weeks," he says with a disgusted look on his face.

"Good, I may have something for you," I tell him, knowing Declan won't have an issue with her other best friend watching over her.

"Gather everyone into the conference room," I tell him.

"They are already waiting, except for Declan, we can't reach him," Heath says, worried.

"I know where Declan is, don't worry, he's fine," I say and watch his shoulders relax.

I follow behind Heath as we walk to the conference room. Heath takes a seat next to Mya, and all three of them look at me.

"Kim has been found," I say, and the room erupts.

"What?"

"Where is she?"

"Where was she?"

"How is she?"

I hold up my hand, and they quiet down.

"Last night, as Michelle and I were getting ready to leave her office, Kim showed up at her door before she collapsed," I tell them, looking at all three.

"I called 9-1-1, and we got her to the hospital. She's been beaten really badly, the doctor had to wire her jaw shut to fix it properly. She has a broken arm, and bruises over her entire body. She was also drugged."

"Oh my God, Kimmy," Heath says with tears in his eyes.

I continue, "The doctors have her in a medically induced coma to help her heal and flush out all the drugs in her system."

"Do they know when they plan to pull her out of it?" Mya asks.

"Not yet. She's currently in the ICU, and there will be someone with her at all times. We don't know who did this or how she escaped," I say, watching Frankie as he clenches his fists.

"Can I be the first one to watch her?" Frankie asks.

"No. Since Heath is on light duty for the next three weeks, he will take the day shift, and Declan will take the night shift, which is where he was last night and why he is not here. I sent him home to sleep while Michelle is currently staying with Kim," I say.

"What do you need us to do, Boss?" Mya asks.

"I need you and Frankie to pull every CCTV footage, starting with the State Building, and see if you can follow to see where she came from," I tell them both, and they nod.

"Do not be afraid to go visit her, and let her know you are there for her, but be mindful of the visiting hours. They are sticklers for the rules in the ICU ward," I tell them.

"Heath, go head to the hospital, and Michelle will bring you up to speed."

He nods and leaves the room.

"Why are you only putting two people to take turns watching over her, Boss," Frankie asks, sounding hurt that he wasn't chosen.

"So as not to overwhelm the nurses. If they only have to remember two agents for day and night shifts, then when they don't see them, they will know something is wrong," I say sternly.

"That makes perfect sense, Boss. We already lost her once and whoever took her is still out there," Mya says, looking pointedly at Frankie.

"You're right," he says, with resignation in his voice.

"Let's go get some CCTV footage," Mya says before adding, "And find this fucker."

I can't help the grin that crosses my face as they walk out, but now I understand what Declan was talking about with Frankie. He is definitely going to cause issues as soon as their relationship comes to light.

Two hours later, there is a light knock on my door. I look up from what I'm doing.

"Boss, you need to come see this," Mya says, standing in my doorway.

I get up from my seat, walk around my desk, and follow her to the conference room.

The big TV is on, and she walks over to her laptop to push play. I watch as Kim stumbles out of the woods on the other side of the big parking lot of the State Building. She keeps looking over her shoulder as she's slowly making her way to the building door. I can see how exhausted she is, but she keeps moving.

"We know once she goes through the doors, where she goes," Mya says.

"What is on the other side of those woods?" I ask, never paying attention before.

"Not sure, Boss, but also we don't know which direction she came from in the woods," Frankie says.

"Well let's go over there and see if we can find any tracks to help us," I tell both of them.

They nod, getting up from their seats and heading out of the office to the parking lot.

I drive the three of us over there, parking the car next to where we saw Kim emerge. I pull a map out of my glovebox and grab a pen from my shirt pocket. Everyone gets out of the car and walks over to the edge of the woods.

Lucky for us, the ground is fairly wet due to the small amount of rain we have received over the last month. I immediately spot Kim's footprints, which isn't hard since she was barefoot.

As we follow her tracks, I mark the route on my map. Three miles in, we come to a farmhouse. I send Mya over there to see if it's occupied and if they happened to see anything.

Frankie and I continue following Kim's footprints, this time, they lead us to the barn on the property. I open the door to an empty barn. There is nothing here, almost like it hasn't been used in a very long time.

I see a disturbance in the dust on the floor and find a spot where Kim was laying. Her tracks lead to the back of the barn, where the wood is rotted, and there is a hole for someone small to climb through.

I stick my head out the hole and see her footprints immediately.

"This isn't where she was held," I say. "I think this is where she stopped to rest," I add before walking back toward the front of the barn.

Mya meets us out front with the homeowner, an older lady, probably in her sixties, if I had to guess.

"Boss, this is Mrs. Horne. She owns this property," Mya says.

"Mrs. Horne," I acknowledge her. "I apologize for invading your property," I tell her.

"It's fine, Agent. I don't come out this way and haven't since my Earl passed away," she tells us.

"Did you by chance see anything the other night?" I ask her.

"As I was telling your Agent here, I'm normally in bed by seven. If your Agent was here, I didn't know," she tells us, with sincerity in her eyes.

"Thank you for your time, Mrs. Horne, we will leave you," I tell her, and she nods, turning around and walking back toward the main house.

I walk around the barn to where the hole in the back of the barn is and quickly find Kim's tracks again.

We walk another three miles before we turn back around to go back to the car. I have marked the route on the map and will study it once we are back in the office to see if there is anything else around that could help us.

After looking over the map in that area, we found there is a road that comes out on the back of the woods where we were. Our plan is to see if we can pick up Kim's trail on the other side of those woods tomorrow.

"Make sure to wear comfortable hiking clothes," I tell Mya and Frankie before adding, "I want to start early, so let's meet here at seven am."

"Yes, Boss," they both say in unison.

I leave the office and head to the hospital to pick up Michelle and make sure Declan slept.

When I get to Kim's room, the doctor is there, and I hear him say, "I would like to wait the full six weeks to allow her jaw to heal before pulling her out of the induced coma, and even then, I will be doing it slowly."

"Six weeks?" Declan and Heath say together.

"This will give her body time to heal as well, so when she wakes up, there is a good chance her cast will be off her arm, the bruises will have faded, and her jaw will no longer be wired, though it may take her some time to start talking."

"That's fine, Doctor, if this is what you think is best," Michelle says.

"I do," he says as he looks at me.

I nod, and he leaves the room.

Six weeks of finding out what happened to Kim on our own. I had hoped they would bring her out sooner so she could possibly help us, but I also don't disagree with the doctor. She does need to heal.

I look over at Declan and see he looks a little better, though I can see the worry in his eyes as he looks at Kim.

"Six weeks is a long time, but this is what is best for Kim, plus we don't know how much she will be able to tell us anyway," I tell them all and watch their heads nod.

Heath has tears falling down his face as he looks at his best friend lying on the bed.

"Heath," I call out, and he looks over at me. "Go home, get some rest, and be back here at eight am to take over the day shift."

He nods at me before squeezing Michelle's hand while looking at Kim, then he nods slightly at Declan before walking out the door.

"Have you eaten?" I ask Declan.

"Yes, Sir. I grabbed a sandwich before I came in," he tells me, standing on the other side of Kim's bed.

The door opens, and we all look to see who it is, as Mya and Frankie both walk in. I hear Mya gasp as she takes in Kim's battered body.

She quickly composes herself, but I notice Frankie can barely look at Kim.

"How is she doing, Boss?" Mya asks.

"The doctors are going to keep her in a coma for six weeks to allow for everything to heal before they slowly bring her out," I tell them.

"Six weeks?" Frankie whispers, looking down at his hands.

"Yes. This will give her arm and jaw time to heal properly before they take everything off," I say, relaying what the doctor told us.

"Hopefully, we can catch the monster who did this to her before she wakes up," Mya says, with venom in her voice.

That would be nice, I say to myself internally, though I don't think that's how it's going to go.

"For now, we just keep backtracking her steps and see if it will lead us anywhere," I tell them.

They both nod and then I grab Michelle's hand, leading her out of Kim's room as we follow behind Frankie and Mya, leaving Declan alone with Kim for the night.

Chapter Thirteen

UNKNOWN

"Where the hell is she?" I grunt out as I look around the basement where I keep all the women. I take in their faces and see sheer panic.

The chair where I had her handcuffed around the pole is empty, except for the handcuffs, which are lying empty on the floor.

"WHERE IS SHE?" I scream out.

All the other women in the room fold into themselves, shaking.

I grab one of the females off the bed closest to me, drag her over to the chains, and chain her hands up above her head. I begin to punch her hard, needing the release of my anger.

I barely register her screams as I continue using her as a punching bag.

I can't believe she got away. None of them have ever gotten away from me. The only way they leave me is through death. How could this happen?

I need to find her. She couldn't have gotten far. She must be hiding in the woods. The drugs in her system wouldn't have allowed her to get far.

With that knowledge, I allow my anger to dissipate. My mind already forming a plan to find her, I stop punching my latest release, only to find my prey is dead.

I laugh as I take in the battered and broken woman hanging in front of me.

I can hear the sniffling from the other women in the room, including sweet Marabel. The fear is potent in the room, and it makes my cock ache for release.

I leave the dead woman hanging, make my way over to Marabel. I unzip my pants, pull my cock out, grab her by her legs, open them up, and slam into her as she screams.

"Oh, my sweet Marabel," I grunt in her ear as I continue to thrust hard in her tight pussy. "You are going to learn to love what I give you."

I grunt my release inside her. I stand up, tucking my cock back in my pants, having both of my urges sated. Now it's time to find my prey and bring her back home.

I will break her, and she will pay for running away.

I walk out of the basement to go hunting.

Chapter Fourteen

DECLAN

Six weeks later

Today is the day the doctor is going to take out the wire from her jaw, take her cast off, and slowly bring her out of the medically induced coma. He informed us she won't wake up immediately. This will be a slow process and could take either a few days or weeks for her to wake up. Once they stop the medication to keep her under, the rest will be up to her.

I've been here all night, like every night, but I have no intentions of going home this morning until I know she is okay.

Eric, Frankie, and Mya have been tracking her footprints, but still have no idea where she came from. They had tracked her footprints in the woods for nearly twenty miles until the heavy rainstorm washed all traces away. They were able to get some CCTV footage from some nearby facilities in some of the areas tracking her timeline. So far, it looks like she had escaped possibly a week to a week and a half before she showed up at the morgue.

The team is all here, waiting in the waiting room for the doctor to come back and tell us when everything is complete, and she's back in her room.

I end up dozing off in the chair until Heath shakes me to wake up as the doctor walks toward us.

"Agent Santiago is back in her room. Everything seems to have healed very well based on the x-rays," he tells us before continuing, "As we said before, we have stopped the medication that kept her in a coma, so now everything is on her own time."

"Thank you, Doctor," Eric tells him, and we all nod our heads in thanks.

"She's back in her room, and we will continue to monitor her closely, but should she wake up, please alert a nurse immediately," he tells us.

"Yes, Doctor," we all say in unison, and I release the breath I wasn't aware I was even holding this whole time.

We all walk back into Kim's room together, and I quickly notice her cast is gone from her arm, her jaw no longer has a wire poking out of her mouth. Her bruises disappeared a couple of weeks ago, and right now, she just looks like she is sleeping peacefully.

"Do you think she will remember anything when she wakes up?" Frankie asks.

Kim's heart rate accelerates at that moment as the machine begins to beep loudly. The nurse comes running in, and I call out, "What's wrong?"

Her heart rate immediately drops back to normal, almost as if she heard my voice.

"Everything is fine, it seems she may be trying to wake up. She hears you all talking," she tells us, jotting some notes down on Kim's chart. "Continue talking to her, that may help pull her out of the coma," she adds before walking out of the room.

"Okay, let's not overwhelm Kim too much before she has even opened her eyes," Eric starts. "Declan, go home and get some sleep. Mya and Frankie, we have more videos to track down. Let's leave Michelle and Heath here, and they will let us know if there are any changes."

Both Michelle and Heath nod their heads, and I follow Mya, Frankie, and Eric out of Kim's room, but not before turning to look at her one more time. Michelle catches my eyes and gives me a slight nod, letting me know she's got Kim.

I leave and make my way home to get a few hours of sleep before I go back to the hospital. Though I want Kim to wake up, I just pray she waits until I get back, because selfishly, I want to be the first person she sees.

At five pm, I'm walking into the hospital and make my way to the elevator that will take me to the ICU floor. When the elevator doors open, Frankie comes barreling out, looking pissed.

"Hey, what's going on? Is Kim okay?" I ask.

"Heath kicked me out of her room."

"Why?"

"He says that I seem to be the only one whose voice causes her heart rate to go up. The machines started going off, and the nurse had to come in. I mean, did he ever take into consideration that maybe she wants to talk to me," he says with a huff in his voice.

"What did the nurse say?" I ask him.

"She thinks Kim is trying to wake up, and she believes she has something to say, but the meds are still in her system," he says, and I nod.

"Well, I'm going to go up and relieve Heath, what are you going to do tonight?" I ask him.

"I'm going to go to the gym. I need to work out on the bag, I'm feeling very frustrated with everything."

"Okay, see you later," I tell him, getting into the elevator, curious to hear Heath's thoughts.

I get up to Kim's room, and I walk in to see Heath upset.

"What's going on, Heath? I just saw Frankie getting off the elevator, and he looked upset. What happened?"

"That man," he huffs. "There is seriously something wrong with him," he says.

"What happened?" I ask again.

"He came in here talking about what he, Mya, and Eric have found so far, and her heart monitor went ballistic. The nurse had to run in here, and I had to soothe her, letting her know I was here. I told him to leave."

"He seems to think that maybe she wants to say something to him," I tell him.

"It's possible. The nurse said something similar, but her heart monitor never goes ballistic when anyone else is in here, and I'll be damned if he gives my girl a heart attack on top of everything else she has been through," Heath says.

"Interesting," I mutter to myself, but Heath hears me.

"It is indeed. I think there is more to it, but we won't know until Kimmy wakes up," he says, looking down at her, before adding, "Now would be good, missy."

We both look at her, but she gives no indication she heard him. He shakes his head, then says, "I will leave you, but if she wakes, call me immediately."

"I will, don't worry," I tell him.

Heath walks out of the room, and I take the seat next to her bed.

"Hey, beautiful," I whisper to her. "I really wish you would wake up. I want to look into those beautiful chocolate eyes of yours," I tell her as I grab her hand.

There is no movement, and I can't help the sigh that escapes my lips. I continue to sit there, holding her hand, talking to her, begging her to wake up, but she just lays there peacefully.

I wonder if Frankie is right and if he is who she wants to talk to. Why does she only react to his voice, but not the rest of us? I internally question.

The night continues on with the nurses coming in and out throughout the night, and I continue to sit there, waiting for a sign, anything from Kim to let me know she knows I am there.

Heath and Michelle come in at eight. "Any changes?" Michelle asks, and I shake my head no.

I watch as both their faces fall, but then Michelle looks at me and says, "Go home and get some sleep, Declan. We will call if there are any changes."

"Okay," I say, unable to keep the melancholy out of my voice.

Michelle squeezes my arm before turning back to the bed and Kim.

I leave and head home to get a few hours of sleep, praying I get a call. I just want her to wake up and know that she is okay.

Chapter Fifteen

KIM

I can hear Declan talking to me, but I can't move anything. My body feels like it's weighted down. The darkness keeps sucking me under, no matter how hard I try to open my eyes. He's begging me to wake up, and I want to, but I can't.

There is a beeping sound, but I can't place it. I want to open my eyes and see what it is, but I can't. Why can't I wake up? Why can't I move my body? What happened to me? I try to remember, but my head starts to pound until the black abyss pulls me under again.

I can hear Michelle and Heath talking, but I'm not sure what they are talking about.

"I don't understand why she is not waking up?" Heath asks.

"The doctor said it would be in her time, plus her body needs to process the medication out of her system," I hear Michelle say.

Doctor? Medication? I'm so confused. I want to speak, to ask the questions, but my mouth feels like it's glued shut. Nothing wants to work right now. I allow the abyss to pull me under again, in hopes the next time I come to, I can open my eyes.

I don't know how much time has passed since I heard Heath and Michelle talking, but my mind listens for any sounds, picking up the annoying beeping sound. I need to know what that noise is.

I try to open my eyes, and this time, they open. The room is dark, safe for a light going around the border of the walls at the top. I look over and see a monitor with a red blinking light and numbers that make no sense to me.

I turn my head to the other side, and there in a chair beside my bed is Declan. His eyes are closed as his head is leaned back against the chair. I look down and see his hand in mine, and I give him a little squeeze.

His head pops up as he looks at me.

"Oh my God, Kim, you're awake," he says, with so much love and adoration in his voice. "How are you feeling?"

I try to talk, but my throat is so dry. I croak out, "Water."

"Let me get the nurse first, babe," he tells me as he walks hastily to the door.

My eyes are burning, so I close them for a second as I get my bearings. He said he was going to get a nurse, so I must be in the hospital, but why? What happened?

I hear the door open again, and I open my eyes to see Declan smiling and the nurse coming in behind him.

"Nice to see you awake, Agent Santiago, how are you feeling?" she asks sweetly.

"Water," I croak out again, as it seems to be the only thing I can say.

"Absolutely, dear," she says, lifting the cup with a straw. "Now take little sips," she tells me as she holds the cup and straw.

The taste of the cool water soothes my throat and though I want more, I do as she says and take little sips.

"Perfect. How do you feel now?" she asks me.

"Tired," I croak out.

"Well, that's to be expected. Your body is going to be tired as you adjust to waking up," she tells me with a smile.

"Why am I here?" I ask, and I see the nurse look over at Declan, so I turn my head, but I must have done it too fast because immediately I am dizzy and have to close my eyes.

"Hey, rest. We can talk about all this once you've recovered," I hear Declan tell me, and though I think I nod, I allow the black abyss to take me again.

The next time I wake up, the room is bright from the sunlight, and it takes my eyes a few minutes to adjust. When they are finally adjusted, I see the whole team and Michelle in my room.

"Hey," I say, sounding weak.

"Hey," Michelle says, tears pooling in her eyes.

"Why are you crying? What happened?" I ask.

"I'm just so happy to see you awake," she tells me as she grips my hand, giving it a squeeze.

"Do you remember anything?" Eric asks, and I look over at him.

I try to think, but the headache that is starting to pool at my temple does not allow me. I rub my temples, but Eric is the one who says, "Don't worry about it, things will come to you when you are better. Just know you are in the hospital and being taken care of."

Before I can respond, the door opens, and in walks an older gentleman in a white coat.

"Agent Santiago, so glad to see you awake. I am Doctor Sava, and I'm going to check you over, okay?"

I nod because I don't know what else to do.

"Can you all please wait outside while I examine the patient?" he asks the team, and they all nod as they form a line to walk out the door.

"I'll be right outside," Michelle says, squeezing my hand again, then following Eric out, and I watch the door close.

"How do you feel?" he asks me.

"I have a headache, and my throat hurts, but other than that, I think I'm okay," I tell him honestly.

"Do you remember what happened?"

I shake my head no, then say, "Every time I try to remember, but my head starts pounding."

"Don't force the memories, they will come when they are ready. I will have the nurse bring you some medication for the headaches, but allow your memories to come on their own," he tells me as he runs his tests.

"Okay, Doc," I tell him, then I ask, "When will I be able to go home?"

"It will depend on you. I will have the nurse get you and see how far you can walk. I will also have food brought in, though you probably won't eat a whole lot, I just want to make sure you are able to keep it down."

I nod in understanding as he is telling me these things.

"If all goes well, you can probably go home in a week," he adds, checking my arm and having me squeeze his fingers.

"A week?" I croak out.

"Only if everything goes well," he says again as he jots some notes down, before he looks at me and says, "Don't overdo it, and rest when you are tired. That is the only way you are going to be able to leave."

I nod, feeling disappointed that I can't go home now.

Doctor Sava opens the door, and I hear him tell the team they can come in and see me, but not to overstimulate me.

Michelle is the first one through the door, with Heath coming in closely behind her. They each take up a side as Mya, Frankie, Declan, and Eric stand at the wall in front of my bed.

"So what have I missed?" I ask.

I see a lot of funny looks going around, but then Heath says, "Mya has a McHotty."

"Huh?" I ask, confused, looking over at Mya, who rolls her eyes at Heath, but I can see the smile on her face.

"His name is Shane Mcguire and he is a Homicide Detective in Boston."

"Boston?" I ask.

"We will tell you all about it another time, for now, you need to rest, and these guys need to get back to work," Eric says, and I can only frown.

How long was I out? I wonder as I chew on my bottom lip.

"Glad to see you awake," Frankie says, and something about that causes me to tense, but I only nod.

I look over at Declan and catch him looking at me. I give him a small smile, and he gives me a nod.

Everyone leaves the room except Heath and Michelle.

"Tell me the truth, how long have I been here?"

"You've been in the hospital just over six weeks," Shelly tells me.

"What? Why?" I ask.

"That is what you are going to have to tell us," Shelly says, giving a pointed look at Heath.

"You can't tell me what happened? Why not?"

Shelly sighs and says softly, "Because we don't know what happened."

"How could you not know what happened to me? Was I in an accident?" I ask.

"Kim, you were missing for almost a month, before you showed up at the morgue and collapsed," Shelly tells me.

"We don't know where you've been, sweetie," Heath chimes.

I look at them both, stunned, unable to process what I am hearing. *I was gone for almost a month? How?*

"We are just grateful you are back safe, and now you are awake," Shelly tells me.

"Wait, what about your wedding?" I ask as that should be coming up soon if I have correctly done the math.

"We have postponed it until you are one hundred percent better," Shelly says.

"No, Shell, you shouldn't have to postpone your day," I tell her.

"It's fine. It's not like I'm not already married to the man," she tells me as she waves her hand. "The most important thing is you getting better and getting out of this hospital."

I nod, feeling like all of this is my fault somehow. I can't quell the guilt I'm feeling or the emotions that seem to overtake me, learning it's been over two months since the team has seen me, and no one can tell me what happened.

The tears start to flow down my face, and I can't stop them.

"Oh, honey bun, don't cry," Heath says.

"Kim, what's wrong?" Shelly asks at the same time.

"I don't know. Everything is...it just seems...so overwhelming," I stutter as I cry harder.

"It's okay. You're here, we are here, everything is going to be fine," Shelly says.

But I can't help the feeling in the pit of my stomach that she's wrong. Everything is not going to be fine. I just don't know why.

Chapter Sixteen

UNKNOWN

Oh, I knew Kimberly would be strong. Even after the beatings to her body and the drugs in her system, she still managed to run as far as she could. She had no clue where she was, but still managed to find her way to the State Building and into the morgue.

The doctors had placed her in a medically induced coma, but it seems after six weeks, my fighter has finally woken up.

I wonder if she will remember anything, or will I get to start a new game. I clasp my hands together, rubbing them with glee at the thought of starting all over with her.

I try to visit her, but there is always someone with her. The FBI boss doesn't want anyone in there without one of their own.

At night, her not-so-secret romance stays with her in the hospital room, and during the day it's the medical examiner and the gay nut.

She's never alone, and it pisses me off.

Unfortunately, these last few weeks, my anger has gotten the best of me, and I've killed three more women. I'm currently filling a hole that I just buried them all in, where they will not be found for many years.

I will need to go back on the hunt to replace what I've destroyed.

Sweet Marabel is still breathing, as I only take my rage on her pussy. Thinking about it has me hard, and as soon as I bury these cunts, I will go and soothe that ache.

I never got the opportunity to try Kimberly out, but make no mistakes, when I get her back, and I will. This time, I will make sure she never leaves unless it's like these bodies.

I finish filling the hole, ensuring the dirt is smooth and compacted, then I spread out all the leaves and sticks, pressing some of them into the ground to keep the area from looking like it's been disturbed.

I need to make a plan for when Kimberly is released from the hospital. That will be the only way I'll be able to get her back.

Chapter Seventeen

DECLAN

When I get back to Kim's room, I see she is sleeping again. I look at Heath and Michelle and see they have worried looks on their faces.

"What's wrong?" I ask immediately.

"Nothing," Shelly says with a sigh.

"She had a rough day today," Heath says.

"What do you mean she had a rough day? What happened?" I ask again.

Michelle sighs, then tells me, "Kim knows that she was missing for almost a month and had been in the hospital for over six weeks. She didn't take it well."

"Why did you tell her?"

"Because she wanted to know what happened to cause her to be in the hospital, and we had to be honest and tell her we didn't know," she admits, and I can't help the sigh that leaves me.

"What did she do?"

"She cried until she passed out," Heath says quietly.

"I get it, but I wish you hadn't told her yet," I can't help saying. "We should have eased her into the truth."

"You know she wasn't going to have any of that. She would rather know up front, deal with it, and then move on," Michelle says, chastising me.

"I know," I admit reluctantly, while shaking my head.

"It's fine, I needed to know the truth," Kim says from her bed with her eyes still closed. "It will just take me a little while to accept that I haven't been around," she adds.

"Does she remember anything?" I mouth to Michelle, but she shakes her head no.

"How are you feeling?" I ask.

"Drained," she answers honestly.

"That's to be expected, you haven't been up and about for over a month, maybe tonight we can get you walking a little bit," I suggest, and her eyes open, looking at me as if that's the best thing she's heard all year.

I chuckle, before saying, "I guess that's a yes?"

"Yes. I want to go home sooner than later, but the doctor told me, I need to be able to walk and keep food down before he will consider releasing me," she says with a sigh.

"Okay then, we start slow. First, we will walk around the room, then we get you some soup," I suggest, and she nods.

"Good," I say, giving her a big smile.

"That's perfect, and tomorrow, we will do the same," Michelle says, and Heath nods.

"Don't worry, sweetie, we will have you out of here and back home in no time," Heath tells her, and she smiles at him.

"Sounds good to me," she replies.

Heath and Michelle leave the room, and I help Kim sit up in the bed with her feet dangling over the edge.

"We are going to take this slow," I tell her as I pull the metal rolling pole that is currently holding her IV bags out from between the bed and monitors, so she doesn't hurt herself when she stands.

I help her to her feet, holding her around the waist until she is able to stand on her own. Her breathing is hard from the strain of trying to stand up.

When she tries to move, her legs buckle at her knees, but I quickly grab her, not allowing her to fall.

"Guess I'm weaker than I thought," she says shyly, with a small smile.

"Not even close," I inform her. "You've been lying in a bed for over six weeks, this is to be expected," I add.

"I guess my mind and body are just not in sync at the moment. My mind says I can do this, and my body doesn't seem to want to cooperate," she says with a sigh.

"Don't put so much pressure on yourself. I've already told you that we will take this slow. One foot at a time, one step at a time," I tell her.

She nods, and then slides one foot in front of her. I continue holding her around her waist to ensure she doesn't fall. She slides the other foot in front of her, and little by little, we make the short walk to the window.

By the time we get there, she is winded and needs a break. I leave her holding onto the windowsill to get her a chair to sit in.

Once I have her seated by the window, I ask her, "How do you feel besides winded?"

"A bit tired, to be honest. I didn't realize walking was going to be exhausting."

"You did great," I tell her, giving her the confidence I know she needs.

She nods, then says, "I'm not looking forward to walking back to the bed. I know it's a short distance, but it feels like a marathon."

"Do you want me to carry you back to bed?" I ask her, loving the thought of holding her in my arms.

She thinks about that for a few minutes, and I can see her wavering, but then she shakes her head, "No, I need to do this if I want to go home," she says with a sigh.

She stands up out of the chair, and this time, I follow behind her, keeping the IV pole from getting close to her feet.

She slides her feet all the way to the bed. Once her hands are on the bed, I help her to turn around, placing her butt on the bed, before scooting in. I put the IV pole back where it was, straightening the lines out, before covering her back up with the blankets.

"Thank you," she tells me, and I can't help the smile that crosses my face.

"No need to thank me. I will always be here for you no matter what," I tell her.

"What happened to me?" she asks quietly.

"I don't know, babe. I went to your house to pick you up for dinner, and...." I can't help to pause as I choke up with the memory of that night. "You were gone. Just gone," I tell her softly, with tears forming in my eyes as I look up at her.

"I'm so sorry," she tells me, tears pooling in her eyes.

"I looked everywhere for you. Every night, I was on the streets, hitting up our contacts for any information, and nothing. I feel like I failed you," I admit to her quietly.

"You did not fail me. I know you, Declan, and I know you would have done everything you could to find me. I just wish I could remember," she says with frustration in her voice.

"You will, when it's the right time. Don't force it," I tell her, not wanting her to be any pain.

She nods, understanding what I'm saying, as she closes her eyes.

"How about if I call in an order for some soup from your favorite restaurant?" I ask her.

"That would be lovely, thank you," she answers without opening her eyes.

I allow her to rest as I send Heath a text,

> **Can you pick up a bowl of Kim's favorite soup from Garofino's?**

> **Anything for my girl.**

I smile because even though I know I have nothing to worry about when it comes to Heath, she will always be my girl.

The nurse comes in to check on Kim, who is now sleeping.

"How is she doing?" she asks in a whisper.

"She walked a bit from the bed to the window and back, and I think it wore her out. I have some soup being delivered, hopefully that will help get her strength back up," I quietly reply to her.

She nods. "Good. Let me know if you need anything," she says as she jots down notes in Kim's chart before leaving the room.

I listen to Kim's soft, even breaths, feeling more relaxed now that she is awake and able to move around a bit, but I won't be completely relaxed until she is at home with my arms wrapped around her.

Twenty minutes later, Heath comes in with a bag, and I know he brought more than soup. As if Kim could smell the food, her eyes pop open, and she looks around until they settle on the bag.

"Garofino's?" she asks.

"Of course, boo. I wouldn't just get you soup from anywhere," Heath says, sounding as if that would be the worst thing in the world.

"You always know how to take care of me," she tells him with a smile.

"Well, if it wasn't for me, you'd probably be stuck with the bland hospital soup, and we couldn't have that. We need to get you out of here," he tells her.

"Hey, I do believe I sent you a text," I say, offended he's taking my credit for the soup.

"Oh, calm your tits, big man, we know I'm the one with the brains, and that's why I brought you dinner too," he tells me with a smile.

I can't help the look of disbelief that crosses my face at him talking to me like that, but Kim just laughs, and I can't help the smile that forms on my face hearing her laugh.

"Ahh, that's better, babe. We've missed that laugh," Heath says as he pulls her soup and spoon out of the bag.

I pull the tray up to her bed and adjust her bed to help her sit up so she can eat.

She moans with the first bite, and my cock instantly hardens at the sound. I try to feign indifference with Heath in the room, but I can't hide the evidence of how she affects me.

"Go slow, we don't want you getting sick," I tell her, and she nods.

Heath hands me the bag with the food he got me, and I give him my thanks as I take out the spaghetti with meat sauce dish and garlic bread. I don't know when the last time I ate a real meal was.

Heath has his own meal, and we all sit in Kim's room eating together.

"Are there any cute male nurses here?" he asks.

"Not that I've seen. Only female nurses have come in here, and I haven't been outside the room yet. Are you not seeing Chris anymore?" she asks with a pout.

"Oh, we are. I was thinking about you, sugar cakes," he says as he looks over at me.

I say nothing, though inside, I'm seething at his implications of finding her a man.

Kim laughs before telling him, "When are you going to stop trying to get me to date?"

"Never. I know there is someone out there for you, and we will find him."

I continue sitting here in the chair, pretending not to be interested in their conversation but wishing I could claim her as mine.

Then I hear Heath say, "Unless you have already found your man?"

Kim just says, "Hmmm, interesting point," before taking another spoonful of soup and then calling it quits.

"Interesting, how?" he asks, but she closes her eyes.

"Thanks for the soup, babe, but I'm getting really tired now," she says with a yawn.

I get up and lower the bed, making sure she is comfortable before she falls back asleep.

Heath looks at her with a frown before looking at me.

"It's going to take her some time to get her strength back. She walked to the window and then had to take a break before walking back to the bed. It wore her out," I admit, looking down at her.

He frowns as he nods his head. "Okay, I will make sure she does some walking during the day, and I'll also have her do some yoga for strengthening," he states.

"That sounds like a plan, and I think she will appreciate it. She really wants to get out of the hospital," I admit to him, and he nods.

"I get it, I wouldn't want to stay in this drab, cold room either. It can be so depressing," he says dramatically.

"Thanks again for picking up the food. I didn't want to leave her here alone," I whisper to him.

"Pfft, it wasn't a problem. I was happy to help," Heath says, waving his hand, but I could see the smile on his face.

"I'll just see if the nurse can put this in their refrigerator until tomorrow," he says of Kim's soup, "And I'll be back tomorrow morning."

"Thanks again, Heath," I tell him as he walks towards the door.

"Take good care of my girl. I don't want to see her hurt," he says before walking out of the room.

Does he know or was he fishing? I internally ask myself, but then realize I don't care one way or the other. Kim is mine, and I want the world to know it.

Chapter Eighteen

KIM

I wake up to the sun shining in the room. I'm surprised to see I slept through the night. I stretch as much as I can with the IV in my arm, feeling better than I have since I officially woke up.

"Good morning, Beautiful," Declan says, and I can't help but smile at him.

"Good morning."

"How are you feeling today?"

"Better than I have. Maybe doing that little bit of walking yesterday and the soup was exactly what I needed," I tell him.

"Good. Heath will be here shortly, and he plans to have you walk some today and try to do some light yoga to help build your strength up."

"Okay, that sounds good," I tell him.

"Tonight, we will walk a little more and see how far you get," he tells me.

"Are you planning on being a drill sergeant about this?" I ask, quirking my eyebrow up at him.

"No, we just want to help you with your goal of getting out of here sooner rather than later," he tells me with a deadpan look before adding, "Unless you would rather stay here?"

"No, no. I will do the extra work, anything to get back in my own bed," I concede, knowing I'm going to hurt, but he's right, if I want to get out of here, I need to meet the doctor's criteria.

"Good, sugar cakes, because we are going to work and sweat, but first, I'm going to need you to brush your teeth. You are definitely not bringing the boys into this yard with that breath," Heath tells me, and I feel mortified as I cover my mouth.

"Oh my God, I feel ashamed, I never thought about my hygiene. See, this is why I need to go home," I say out loud, horrified as I look over at Declan.

Why did the man never say anything?

He just shrugs his shoulders, letting me know it doesn't bother him, but it definitely bothers me.

"Don't worry, later we will get you a shower, and then I can do your hair for you so you aren't sleeping on it. Right now, it looks like a rat's nest," Heath tells me brutally.

"Thanks for the honesty," I mutter, not caring that it was done sarcastically.

"You're welcome, babe. I will always be honest," he says. "Now, let's get you up and into the bathroom. This will be your first walk of the day," he tells me with a wink in Declan's direction.

They both help me off the bed, with Declan bringing the IV stand around the bed before handing it off to Heath.

I stand there getting my bearings again when Declan says, "I'll see you both this evening," as he heads for the door.

Heath is pushing me to walk faster, and I can't help the words that come out of my mouth, "How is it that I can't get you to run fast in the park, but here you want to be Speedy Gonzales?"

"Huh? Who?" Heath asks, then says, "Nevermind. I just want to get you into the bathroom before the man of your dreams walks in and sees you in this state and runs away."

"Oh please, you are the one tired of looking at me," I tell him.

"Maybe, or maybe I just don't want to be associated with someone so unkempt. I do have an image to protect," he snarks back, and it makes me push a little harder.

"Unkempt," I mutter. "I've been laying in a hospital bed for weeks, it's not like this is my fault," I tell him.

"Not then, but definitely now, but don't worry, we are going to fix all that," he says as we make it into the bathroom, and he leaves my toiletry bag on the counter. "Do you need to relieve yourself?"

As soon as he asks that question, my bladder decides to make itself known. "Yeah, I do. Shut the door, and if I need any help, I'll call you," I tell him, holding onto the counter of the sink as I walk over to the toilet, pulling the IV stand with me.

As soon as I sit down on the toilet, it's like the dam breaks, and I feel like a lake has just come out of me. Once I finish, I stand, flush the toilet, then sidestep to the sink, where I wash my hands.

I open the toiletry bag Heath brought and pull out a toothbrush and toothpaste. I proceed to brush my mouth wondering when the last time I brushed my teeth was? It had to have been before I disappeared, and with that knowledge, I brush them harder, wanting to ensure they were as clean as possible.

I look in the bag to see what else he brought me, and I see the shampoo, conditioner, body wash, and mouthwash.

I quickly swish some of the mouthwash around. I don't want Heath thinking I did the bare minimum, though maybe that would explain why Declan hasn't kissed me since I woke up. *Why didn't he say anything?* I internally question.

Suddenly, there's a knock at the bathroom door.

"Are you okay in there?" Heath asks.

I spit the mouthwash into the sink, then respond, "I'm fine, just finishing up."

I grab the towel and wipe my mouth and hands before opening the door to a worried-looking Heath.

"Are you okay?" I ask him as I hold on to the IV stand and walk.

"You were in there a long time," he starts to say.

"Well, first, I had to pee in a lake, I thought it would never stop. Then I washed my hands before brushing my teeth because God forbid, I ruin your image. After brushing, for good measure, I used the mouthwash."

"No need to get snarky, I was only trying to be helpful," he says with a huff.

"Mmm hmmm," I hum, not saying anything else.

"Well, it seems you're walking, albeit slowly, but you are walking, so that's good. Ready for some yoga stretching? Since you are still hooked to an IV, I will modify some of these so you can do it while sitting on the bed," he tells me.

"Thank goodness, because I don't think I can get on the floor right now," I tell him as he helps me climb back onto the bed.

He runs me through some arm stretches as well as leg stretches. The nurse comes in and checks on us, giving me an approving nod as she jots down notes in my chart.

When Heath deems us finished, I'm sweating more than I thought I should be for not having done the entire weight of a yoga class. I'm ready for the shower, but then I realize I have the IVs and the IV stand. How am I meant to do this?

"What's wrong, Kimmy?" Heath asks, concern filling his voice.

"I don't know how I'm meant to take a shower?" I say, tears filling my eyes.

I don't know why this is making me emotional, but I want to cry from the unfairness of it all. I just want a hot shower and clean clothes.

"Don't worry, honey, we will take care of this," he says as he pushes the nurse's call button.

Now, why didn't I think of that? I must be more tired than my brain wants to admit.

The nurse comes in. "Is everything okay in here?" she asks as she looks me over when she sees the tears in my eyes.

"Kimmy wants to know how she is supposed to take a shower with the IVs in her arm?" Heath questions for me as I can't find my words right now.

"Oh, thank goodness," she says. "I can fix this. We will just go ahead and take it out, since you are up, I don't think we really need it anymore. Have you gone to the bathroom already?"

I nod. "Yes, ma'am, this morning," I whisper.

"Okay, good. Then we can take this out, and you can have that shower," she says sweetly.

"Thank you so much," I say, allowing her to hear the appreciation in my voice.

"No problem, I'm just glad this was all there was, and you didn't injure yourself doing those stretches," she says with a laugh, and I can't help but to laugh with her.

Once she has the IV out, she helps me walk to the bathroom, shows me where the call button is in the shower, should I need help, then she leaves me to myself.

I turn the water on as hot as I can get it, strip out of the hospital gown and underwear they put me in, grab the bottles of shampoo, conditioner, and body wash that Heath brought, and step under the spray.

Suddenly, I feel like ten pounds of dirt is washing off me and going down the drain. I wash my hair, then condition it, not once, but twice to get the knots out. I grab the body wash next, using the hospital washcloth, and wash my body, needing to wash off whatever unknown that has touched me.

Why did I think that? What unknown could have touched me? I allow the water to cascade over my body as I get an image of a hand, a bloody hand.

I'm trying hard to pull more of the image, to understand it, but it's pulled away by the knock on the bathroom door before it opens.

"Kimmy, are you okay?" Heath calls in.

"Yeah. I'm almost done," I tell him as I turn the water off.

"Okay. I've left you a pair of leggings, underwear, and a t-shirt on the counter for you to put on."

"Thanks, Heath, I appreciate that," I tell him, wishing I could pull the image in my mind up again.

Instead, I grab a towel, dry off, and put on the fresh clothes that Heath brought in, feeling a little more normal than before.

I walk out of the bathroom, taking my time, and find Heath with a brush waiting for me.

"Aww, you look so much better and less pale. These hospital gowns are really not your color," he tells me, helping me to sit on the bed before he brushes my hair for me.

I can't help the chuckle that leaves my lips. "Thank you, Heath, I didn't realize how much I needed that. I guess being confined to a bed, I just forgot the everyday comforts."

"Apparently, Declan did too, if he didn't think about it," Heath says, and I'm not sure what he expects me to say.

"I'm sure it wasn't something high on his priority list," I say, thinking about Declan's work ethic.

"Hmm, maybe not," he says as he continues to brush the knots from my hair, which was made easier by the copious amounts of conditioner I put in it.

The soft strokes of the hairbrush, combined with the stretching and the hot shower, my body goes limp, and apparently, I fall asleep, waking when I smell food. I open my eyes to see Shelly holding bags that I know contain our favorite sandwiches.

"Ahh, food," I say with a smile, noting that Heath braided my hair for me. I touch it, then look over at Heath, smile, and say, "Thank you."

He nods his head.

"Oh, you took a shower and changed," Shelly says excitedly.

"Yes, someone told me I was bad for their image," I say as she hands me the bag with my favorite sandwich.

"Should you be eating that?" Heath asks concerned.

"Won't know until I try it," I tell him with a wink, and though I can tell he is still tense, he does concede with a watchful eye.

I take a bite of the ham and cheese sandwich with mustard, lettuce, and pickles. It tastes like heaven to me, but as with the soup, a couple of bites, and I'm full. I wrap the rest of the sandwich up for later, and I see Heath's shoulders relax.

"I'm fine," I tell him, and he nods.

"Yes, you are, and you will only get better as the days go by," Shelly says, my ever-loving cheerleader with a huge smile on her face.

They both finish their sandwiches and then Shelly says, "Since you ate a little bit, let's try to do some more walking, especially now that you no longer have the IV in."

I nod and gently push off the bed. I'm able to stand with no assistance, and I take that as a win. I walk around the bed and toward the window. My legs don't feel like jelly, and I'm not sure if that's due to the workout Heath and I did earlier or the shower, but I feel good.

I walk to the window with no issue, turn, and smile at my two best friends, who are now doing cheerleader moves, and I can't help but to laugh. I end up needing a chair because I can't stop laughing, which makes Heath and Shelly laugh too.

"Okay, Okay," I say as I try to catch my breath after a few minutes. "I need to pee."

"Can you make it to the bathroom?" Shelly asks.

"I think so, but you can't make me laugh," I tell them both.

I wait a few seconds, hoping my bladder will behave, then I stand up. I must have stood up too fast or something, because I got dizzy, and before I knew it, I felt like I was falling.

I barely hear Shelly and Heath screech, but I feel Heath's arms around me as he keeps me from falling.

"I think I got up too fast," I mutter, as Heath lifts me up back on the bed and Shelly races out to get a nurse. My last thoughts were *I still need to pee* before I blacked out.

Chapter Nineteen

DECLAN

I leave Kim and Heath talking hygiene, and I allow the door to close behind me as I run smack into Frankie.

"Whoo, sorry about that," we both say at the time.

"What's going on?" I ask him.

"I just came to check in on Kim," he tells me.

"She's in there with Heath, he's making her brush her teeth and something about her hair being a rat's nest, so I'm not sure now is a good time to go in there," I tell him.

"Oh, okay," he says and we both head to the elevator together. "How is she doing?"

"She wants to go home, but the doctors aren't ready to release her until she meets some of their basic criteria, such as walking, eating, etc," I say nonchalantly.

"So, no date has been given as to when she will be able to go home?" he asks.

"No, not yet," I tell him, wondering why he's so interested.

As if he is reading my mind, he says, "It would be nice to have her back at work. I miss the whole team being in the office."

I nod, then ask, "How is the search for where Kim was coming along?"

He shakes his head, "Slow. Since the rain washed away her tracks, we've had to rely on places in the area. We found some factory buildings, and most seem to have been abandoned. Eric is requesting search warrants for those properties and buildings so we can rule them out before we move on."

I nod in understanding as we walk out to the parking lot of the hospital. "Let me know if you need an extra pair of eyes to look at something," I offer.

"I'll let Eric know," he calls out as I get to my car.

I give a wave before getting in, starting my car, and heading home to get a few hours of sleep.

The ringing of my phone pulls me out of my slumber. I check the caller ID and see Michelle's name. I quickly answer.

"Michelle, what's wrong?" I ask, knowing she wouldn't call me unless something happened.

"I need you to get here quickly. Kim's had a setback," she says before hanging up.

Setback? What the hell does that mean? My mind whirls with fear as I throw on a pair of jeans and a shirt, not caring that I'm not in uniform. Something has happened to Kim, and I need to get to the hospital.

It took me less than ten minutes to get out of the door and another ten to get to the hospital. When I get up to her room, I find Shelly and Heath crying by the door outside of her room.

"What's happened?" I ask.

"She did fine this morning. Went to the bathroom, brushed her teeth, did some stretching, and then she took a shower. She slept for a little bit when I did her hair, then Shelly brought us sandwiches for lunch. She had a few bites and said she couldn't eat anymore," Heath says as the tears flow down his face.

"I told her to try walking to the window since she no longer had her IV in, and she did. We were cheering her on, and she started laughing hard. We got her a chair to sit in, then when she was done laughing, she said she had to pee," Michelle says.

I can only nod, still waiting to know what caused the setback.

"When she stood up, she collapsed. I caught her before she hit the floor and lifted her up, putting her on the bed while Shelly went to get the nurses."

"The doctor thinks she's having a setback from whatever drugs were in her system. He says that due to the dizziness she experienced and blacking out, she could be having heart issues," Shelly says, crying harder now.

I rub my face with my hands, unable to comprehend. Just then, the door opens, and the doctor calls us into the room.

Walking in, I see Kim on the bed, hooked up to the machines, her IV lines are back in her arm. She's sitting up in her bed, and her eyes turn to me.

"We believe Kim is having a delayed reaction to the drugs that were in her system when she first arrived in the ER. We will have to run more extensive tests, but for the time being, we have put her IV back in to flush fluids through her again. Due to the dizziness and blacking out, we are going to run some tests on her heart to see if there was any damage done. I will also be calling our cardiologist to have a look at Kim," Doctor Sava tells us.

"I'm fine. I just over did it with the laughing," Kim says.

"Maybe, but we need to be certain," Doctor Sava says, "For now, you are to rest and keep your laughing at a minimum."

"Yes, doctor," she says as she rolls her eyes. "By the way, I still need to pee," she adds.

"I'm sure one of your friends will be glad to help you," he says, giving me a wink before leaving the room.

"I'll help you get to the bathroom," Shelly offers. "You scared the shit out of me," she seethes at her.

"And me," Heath adds on.

"I'm sorry, guys. I don't know what happened. I thought I just stood up too fast, that's what it felt like. I got dizzy, then Heath caught me, and then I blacked out," she says.

She looks over at me, I haven't said anything as I keep assessing her, "I'm fine, really," she tells me.

I can only nod. No words can be formed right now. I walk over to the window, looking out, trying to catch my breath and regulate my heartbeat.

Heath grabs a tissue and begins to clean his face. I pretend not to notice, to give him some privacy.

"What type of drugs were found in her system when she came in?" Heath asks, and I forgot he was not aware of that one thing.

I sighed, not sure if I should be the one to say anything.

"Yes, I would like to know that too," Kim says, startling me, and I look over at Michelle.

She shrugs her shoulders, "It's her medical issues," she says, and I nod.

"When you were brought in, the doctors did a blood draw, and the toxicologist found at least two types of dissociative drugs in your system that they were able to identify. I don't know if they ever found a match for the other drugs, as they never told us," I tell her.

"Dissociative drugs, meaning I will probably never know what really happened to me," she whispers as she gets back on the bed.

"I'm sorry," I tell her.

"It's fine, who needs to know what's real and what's made up?" she says, trying to laugh it off, but it falls short because I know that's not what she wants.

I walk over to the bed. "Whatever you remember, no matter what, we will follow that as a lead until we can't," I tell her as I take her hand in mine. "We will find out the truth of what happened to you," I tell her confidently.

She nods, then says, "I think I'm going to take a nap."

We all nod at her, and she closes her eyes.

"Do you want us to stay?" Michelle asks.

"No, I'm here, go home, both of you," I tell them as I watch Kim lying on the bed.

She's not asleep, but I'm sure she's ready for Michelle and Heath to leave. I look back at Michelle. "Thanks for calling me," I tell her, and she nods.

They both leave the room, and I can see her body relax, but her eyes don't open. I didn't agree with giving her this news, but Michelle was right, it's her medical issues at the end of the day, and she has a right to know about it. I'm actually surprised the doctor didn't tell her. Maybe he thought we had, I don't know.

"Go to sleep, baby, I'm right here," I tell her as I sit in the chair next to her bed, and she quietly falls asleep.

An hour later, my phone rings, and it's Eric on the caller ID. Kim stirs, but she's not fully awake. I walk out of the room, deciding to take the call out in the hallway so as not to disturb Kim.

"Hey Eric, what's going on?" I ask as I answer the phone.

"I'm checking to see how Kim is doing. Michelle was upset when I spoke to her, and I want to make sure she's okay."

"Yeah, she went to sleep right after Michelle and Heath left, and she hasn't woken up yet," I tell him.

"I can't believe the doctor never told her about the medications in her system," he says, and I nod, though he can't see me.

"I know. I guess I always assumed she knew after she woke up, but we knew for so long that I never even thought about it," I respond.

"Has he come back to see her?"

"No, nor has the cardiologist that he was planning on bringing in. All we can do is wait, I guess," I tell him before there is a shrill scream coming from Kim's room.

"What the hell? Sorry, Eric, got to go," I say before hanging up the phone and running into Kim's room.

I run in and see Kim holding the hospital phone, tears streaming down her face, as she screams.

"Baby, what's wrong?" I ask, needing to know what the hell happened, but holding her shaking body.

"He's back," she chokes out.

Chapter Twenty

KIM

The shrill ringing of the phone wakes me up. I look around, and Declan is not in here. The phone continues to ring, and I realize it's the hospital room phone.

I lean over and answer it.

"Hello?"

"Kim...ber...ly," the voice on the phone sings out. **"You are a bad girl. You left before we could really play, but I found you. I will bring you back, and you will pay for leaving."**

I can't help the scream that escapes me as images bombard me. That voice, his hands.

"AHHHHHHH.....AHHHHHH...." I scream, holding my head.

Declan comes racing into the room. "Baby, what's wrong? KIM?" he shouts at me as he wraps his arms around my shaking body.

"He's back," I choke out.

I continue to scream as the nurses come in to see what's going on.

"I don't know. All I got from her was 'He's back'," I vaguely hear him say.

"AHHHHHHH.....AHHHHHH..." I continue as the images assault my mind and that voice taunts my memories.

"Kim, please, come back to me, baby," Declan says, but I can't pull out of my own head.

The nurse must have given me something, because all of a sudden, everything begins to fade.

The next time I come to, Declan, Michelle, and Eric are at the foot of my bed having a conversation, but I can't make out what they are saying.

"What's wrong?" I ask, and they all turn to look at me.

"How are you feeling?" Michelle asks.

"My throat is scratchy, and I'm tired," I answer honestly.

"The nurse gave you a sedative to help calm you down," Declan tells me.

"Why?" I ask, but then memories of the phone call come back into my mind, and that voice. "He's back," I say calmly, tears streaming down my face.

They all stare at me, but Declan is the one to ask. "Who's back, baby?"

"I don't know," I tell him honestly. "He always called, taunting me about playing a game. I tried to ignore his calls. He knows where I am," I tell him as I look over at the hospital phone sitting on the table next to the bed.

"What did he say?" Eric asks.

I lie there on the bed, thinking about the call. "He said I was a bad girl, he found me, and he will bring me back, and I will pay for leaving," I tell them as I begin to sob.

"Shh, it's okay. I won't let anyone get to you," Declan tells me, holding me tight. "That man will not get near you again," he vows.

"I can see his hands, they are bloody, and I hurt so much. I can hear screams, but I don't know where or who they are coming from," I tell them all, as my mind flashes with images that I'm unable to piece together.

"Okay, Kim, we need you to calm down. Don't push the memories, just allow them to come on their own," Eric tells me and I already know this, but it's so hard.

"Just rest, sweetie," Shelly says softly, and I can see the worry on her face. I allow my eyes to close once again.

I'm not sure how long I was out, but this time, when I wake up, Declan is the only one in the room with me. I look over to see him sitting in the chair beside my bed, staring at me.

"Hey," I croak out.

"Hey, beautiful, how are you feeling?"

"Okay," I tell him, though I'm not sure how to feel right now.

Just then, the door opens, and in walks a guy with a white coat on. He looks to be in his early forties, maybe late thirties. He has brown hair, brown eyes, and is the same height as Declan as they stand side by side.

"Hello, I'm Doctor Aidan Spencer, I'm the cardiologist. Are you Kimberly Santiago?"

"Yes, Doctor," I tell him.

"It says here, that you stood up from the chair, got dizzy, and blacked out?"

"That's what they tell me. I know I got dizzy, and then I woke up," I tell him.

"Hmmm, okay. I will take a listen to your heart, and then I'll have you do an electrocardiogram, so we can check your heartbeat and see if there are any irregularities. From there, we will decide where to go next once I have those results, okay?"

"Okay, Doctor," I tell him as he sticks the stethoscope in his ears, places the end to my heart and listens while he looks at the monitor to which I'm currently hooked up to again.

He continues to listen to my heart, moving the scope in different places before he takes it off and places the stethoscope around his neck.

The door opens, and a nurse walks in with what I presume is the machine to check my heart. They both work in tandem, putting the white sticky patches on me and then hooking the wires up to those.

I look over and see Declan watching from the window, and I give a small smile.

"Okay, Ms. Santiago, let's see if there is anything going on with your heart," he says, and I lay still looking up at the ceiling.

The test takes about fifteen minutes, and when it's done, Doctor Spencer tears off the paper and looks it over. Then he looks at the nurse, "See if you can schedule her in for an echocardiogram," he says.

Looking over at me, he gives me a small smile, before saying, "There are some irregularities that I would like to look into further, so we are going to schedule you to have an ultrasound of the heart."

"Is there something I should be concerned about, Doctor?"

"I don't think it's anything too serious at the moment, but I would like to ensure that it's also not something that could become serious in the future," he tells me as he pats my hand.

"Okay," I reply because what else is there to say?

The doctor and nurse leave the room with the machine, and I let out a breath I wasn't aware I was holding.

"I'm sure everything is fine, they just want to be cautious" Declan tells me as he slides into the chair next to my bed.

"I'm sure you're right," I tell him softly as worry creeps into my mind.

"Hey," he says, grabbing my hand. "Let's not worry about anything until there is something to worry about."

I nod, though the tears form in my eyes anyway. He stands up from the chair, sitting on the side of my bed, and lifts me into his arms as he pulls me into his chest.

I allow myself a few minutes to cry, but then I pull back, look up at him, and say, "Thank you. I think I'm finally at the overwhelmed stage."

"It's understandable. A lot has happened and now you have these tests, but baby, this is just to ensure there are no other issues down the road."

"But what if there are issues?" I hiccup.

"Then I will be here with you to face each and every one of them. I'm not going anywhere. I told you I love you, and I mean it. I loved you yesterday, I love you today, and I will love you tomorrow," he tells me before leaning down and kissing my lips softly.

The minute his lips touch mine, everything seems to click into place. It feels right, it feels like home. I wrap my arm around his neck, needing to deepen the kiss, and he lets me as our tongues battle each other.

All of a sudden, I hear someone clear their throat and I jump. I never heard the door open.

"Sorry to interrupt," the nurse says, "But it's time to take you for your ultrasound."

I look up at Declan, and he's looking at me. "I'll be right there with you," he whispers, and I nod before he stands up in front of me and I see the tenting in his pants. I can't help the slight chuckle that escapes me, knowing I wasn't the only one affected by that kiss.

Declan moves to the wall away from the bed, trying to hide his hard-on, while the nurse brings in the wheelchair.

The nurse unhooks me from the monitor, grabs the IV bags off the pole, and then she and Declan move me from the bed to the wheelchair. Once I'm in the chair and the IV bags are hooked to the pole on the chair, the nurse looks at Declan and says with a smirk, "Would you like to push her down the hall? We wouldn't want you to inadvertently poke the wrong person."

I can't help the laugh that escapes me as Declan blushes from embarrassment.

"Umm, yeah, I'll push her," he says, and that makes me laugh harder. "Hey, no laughing like that. We don't need you passing out again."

"I'm sorry," I tell him with a smile as I continue to chuckle.

The nurse opens the door, giving us both a big smile while Declan pushes me out of the room in the wheelchair. We follow her down to radiology, where the echocardiogram is to be conducted.

Once there, they have me change into a gown, then I'm placed on a table. The nurse has me roll onto my left side, with my left arm up above my head and my right arm straight on my right side, as she starts the machine.

Declan is waiting in the other room with my wheelchair, as they would not allow him to come in. The nurse who led us down here is currently holding my IV bags up for me.

Doctor Spencer comes in and takes over the ultrasound machine while the nurse moves to stand behind him.

"Okay, Ms. Santiago, let's see what's going on, shall we?" he says as he grabs the wand.

The nurse opens my gown, and the doctor puts the wand under my left breast and starts clicking things on the keyboard.

"Hold your breath for me," Doctor Spencer says, and I do as I'm told.

He clicks some more buttons, moves the wand some more, then has me hold my breath again.

"Okay, we are done. I will look these over and be back to your room with the results soon," he says, getting up from his chair and leaving the room.

The two nurses help me up off the bed, and I walk back to the other room where Declan is waiting with my clothes and wheelchair. He helps me get dressed and seated before the nurse leads us back to the room.

Once I'm situated back on the bed and the nurse leaves, Declan asks, "Did he say anything?"

"No. He just told me he would look them over and then meet me back here to give me the results," I tell him as I close my eyes.

A headache begins to form just above my right eye.

The door opens, and I open one to peek and see who it is. Doctor Spencer comes walking in with a chart and a nurse following behind him.

I open my eyes wider, and he says, "Ms. Santiago, I have your results. You seem to have a small amount of fluid building up around your heart. This could be because of the injuries you sustained. There is not enough fluid to warrant draining or surgery, however, I'm going to have the nurse give you some antibiotics, and we will monitor you to ensure that the fluid doesn't build up further."

I nod my head, though I must look concerned, because he tells me, "It's nothing to worry about right now, hopefully the antibiotics will help the fluid absorb back into the body, and then things should be fine. If that turns out to be the case, I will want to see you back in six months to make sure everything is still good. If that doesn't happen, then we will cross that bridge. For now, just rest and let the medicine do its job."

He pats my hand, nods at Declan, and then leaves the room.

The nurse gives me the antibiotic through my IV. After a few minutes, I can feel the coldness of the medication entering my veins. I shiver with the chill, and Declan looks at me with concern.

"I can feel the medication going in," I say.

He nods, and I lay back, closing my eyes.

Chapter Twenty-One

UNKNOWN

Now that I know she's awake and no longer in a coma, I dial the number on my phone and ask the reception to connect me to her room.

The phone rings, and I almost wonder if she is even in the room when she finally answers.

"Hello?" she says, sounding like she just woke up.

Oh good, I think to myself before I say, **"Kim...ber...ly,"** I sing into the phone. **"You are a bad girl. You left before we could really play, but I found you. I will bring you back, and you will pay for leaving."** I tell her.

The shrill of her scream fills me with so much joy. She may not remember everything yet, but she remembers my voice.

I can hear her bodyguard calling her name, but she continues to scream, and I love it. I hang up the phone before anyone knows I'm on it.

"Oh, to be a fly on that wall," I say out loud as I can't help the laugh that escapes me.

I look over at my newest retrieval, hanging with her arms above her head and her body coated in bruises.

She's not as challenging as I thought she would be. She was fun to play with for a day, but she's not Kimberly. I need the one who got away.

"Have your fun now, I'll be back," I say, still laughing.

Now to figure out a way to get in that hospital room to see her myself without anyone else there.

My phone pings with a text. I look at the message and see the search has been approved, well good thing I already moved my goods to a new location. I laugh as I keep walking.

Chapter Twenty-Two

DECLAN

Kim falls asleep shortly after the nurse administered the medication. I watch her as she sleeps, knowing she needs it. She's been through so much today.

I slide my phone out of my pocket and dial Eric. This time, I stay in the room, not wanting to leave in case another phone call comes in.

"Declan, how's Kim?" he immediately asks as he answers the phone.

"She saw the cardiologist, he did some tests and an ultrasound on her. She has fluid around her heart, but he's given her some antibiotics, and he hopes that will clear it up. She's currently sleeping right now," I tell him.

"Did she remember anything else about the man on the phone?"

"No, Sir," I tell him, while shaking my head.

"We got the search warrant signed off, so Frankie, Mya, and myself will go search those factory buildings and see if we can turn up answers."

"Let me know if you need me there too. I'll be happy to help in the morning," I tell him.

"No, I'll need you to get plenty of sleep. Whoever this is, is not done with Kim, and she's going to need all the protection we can give her," he tells me, and it sends a chill through me as I look over at my woman still sleeping on the bed.

"Okay," I whisper.

"And Declan?"

"Yeah, Boss?"

"Keep your eyes sharp. He knows where she's at and what room she's in. I'm sure he's planning something."

"Got it, Boss," I tell him before we hang up.

I continue looking at Kim, wondering, and not for the first time, what did this maniac do to her?

There's a knock on the door, and then it opens. A gentleman wearing hospital scrubs looks in, "Can I come in and clean, or should I come back later?" he whispers as he takes in Kim's sleeping form on the bed.

"You can come in and clean," I tell the man, who is obviously a custodian for the floor.

He nods and pushes his cart into the room, then makes his way into the bathroom, where he starts to clean.

I go stand by the window where I have access to see everything going on. I can hear the water running in the bathroom and smell the cleaner letting me know he is scrubbing everything down in there.

Kim starts to moan on the bed, turning her head several times. I make my way over to her, just as the man comes out with the trash. He places it in the cart, looks over at Kim, and says, "Do you need a nurse?"

"No, she's just having a bad dream," I say as I try to rouse Kim, but she's in deep.

The man nods, grabs his duster, and dusts everything in the room, including window sills and doors. He then grabs a mop, splashing cleaner on the floor, and mops everything. The antiseptic smell is a little overpowering, but I know they do that for a reason, so I breathe in as little as I can, waiting for it to start to dissipate where it will be tolerable.

Kim is now thrashing on the bed, moaning louder.

"Kim," I call, shaking her shoulders. "Kim, wake up. It's just a dream. KIM!" I yell at her, and that finally does it.

She sits straight up, breathing hard, as she looks around. Her eyes land on the man, who is now by the door, almost finished mopping. She looks around the room, and then her eyes fall on me.

"Hey, are you okay?" I ask her.

"Hmmm, I think so," she whispers, then asks, "What is that smell?"

"Cleaner that the hospital uses. It's a bit overpowering but apparently a necessity," I tell her.

She nods but has a puzzled look on her face.

"Want to tell me about your dream?"

"I don't remember it," she says, looking quizzically like she's trying to figure out what it was. "The smell hit me, that's all I can see to latch onto," she tells me, and I nod.

"It's okay. Are you hungry?" I ask her.

"No, but could you get me some water? I feel like my throat is burning," she tells me.

The man has already left the room with his cart, so hopefully the cleaning smell will follow suit soon. I grab the pitcher of water, the cup, and pour it for Kim. I hand her the cup with a straw.

She drinks slowly, then hands me the cup back when she is finished.

"I need to go to the bathroom," she tells me shyly.

"No problem. Let me grab the IV pole, and then I'll help you off the bed."

I grab the pole, push it to the other side of the bed, and help Kim down.

"Thanks," she tells me as she holds onto the pole, pushing it with her as she walks to the bathroom.

I hear her close the door, and I wait outside, just to make sure she doesn't need me. I hear the toilet flush, then the water in the sink comes on, letting me know she is washing her hands and probably going to brush her teeth as well. I'm sure Heath's earlier words to her this morning are probably echoing in her mind right now.

I chuckle as I walk away from the bathroom door, but not too far away in case she needs me.

The door opens, and she walks out, pushing the IV pole with her.

"Feel better?" I ask.

"Yeah, though I'm still so tired," she says.

"It's probably the antibiotics, they tend to make you drowsy as it fights the infections," I tell her, helping her back on the bed and placing the IV pole back where it goes.

"That's true," she says with a yawn.

"I do think you need to eat something, though," I say with a frown.

She yawns again and says, "Maybe later, right now, I want to sleep," then she closes her eyes.

I text Heath and ask him to bring food for Kim and me since I don't feel comfortable leaving her to go pick anything up.

In true Heath fashion, he comes bouncing into the room with several different bags. This time, Chris is with him.

"Kimmy, I brought you some foooood," Heath sings out, then he stops and pouts. "She's sleeping," he says, looking over at me.

Chris looks at me, shrugs his shoulders, and says, "Hey."

"Hey," I say back, then look at Heath, "Yes, she's sleeping. The doctor has given her some antibiotics, and it's knocking her out. She's only up for a few minutes, then she goes back out, but she hasn't eaten except the couple of bites of that sandwich Michelle brought today, and I know she's going to need something." I tell him.

"What's the antibiotics for?" Heath asked worriedly.

"She has a small amount of fluid around her heart. The doctor thinks it stems from her injuries, so he put her on antibiotics in hopes of the fluid being absorbed back into her body."

"Oh, poor Kimmy," he says, pouting as he looks at her.

"By the way, we need to have another conversation," I tell him.

"I don't need you to tell me," Heath says smugly.

"How do you know? Did Eric tell you?"

"Eric knows?" he gasps.

"Of course, Eric knows. Why would our boss not know?"

"Damn, everyone really be keeping secrets around this bitch," he says thoughtfully.

"What are you talking about? It's not a secret," I say, looking at him like he's crazy.

"Could have fooled me. Not once did anyone say anything to me."

"It just happened today," I say, getting frustrated with him.

"Huh? I thought it was a while ago?" he questions, looking rather dumbfounded.

"The phone call only happened today," I say.

"What phone call?" he asks.

"The one I'm talking about. Wait, what are you talking about, then?" I ask him.

"Don't worry about that, what phone call?" Heath asks, waving the other question away.

"I went out in the hall to take a call from Eric so as not to disturb Kim while she was sleeping. Apparently, the phone in here rang, waking Kim up, and she answered. Turns out it was the person who took her."

"WAIT, WHAT?"

"When she heard his voice, she started screaming. Apparently, it caused her to remember things but only images. The nurses had to give her a sedative to calm her down."

"Whaaattt?' Heath holds out incredulously. "Holy Shit. What did he say? Do we know?"

I nod, "He told her something along the lines of she was a bad girl, he found her, will bring her back, and she will pay for leaving," I tell him.

"Oh, hell no, not my Kimmy. That MFer better stay away from here," Heath says, getting defensive. "He is not taking my girl from me again."

"Well said," Kim mumbles.

"Oh Kimmy, you're awake, babe. I brought you some food. How about we sit you up, you eat, and then we can talk," Heath says, going into mother nurture mode.

I can't help but chuckle at the quickness that he went from angry to sweet talking. Chris looks at me, shakes his head with a smile, and then helps Heath pass out the food.

We all sit, eat, talk until Kim is ready to go back to sleep. Heath tucks her in, while Chris and I gather up the garbage.

Within seconds, Kim is out again, and I catch Heath frowning down at her.

I look over at him and ask, "What?"

"I miss my joyful Kimmy. She's not the same," he whispers, and I can hear him choke on the words.

"Would you be the same waking up in the hospital and finding out you've been missing, not knowing where you were, but knowing something happened, and you can't remember what?"

"No, probably not," he says, shaking his head thoughtfully.

"I don't think any of us would be. We just need to give her time," I say quietly.

"You're right," he says as he takes a deep breath. "I'll bring breakfast in the morning before I come," he says.

"Oatmeal," I say.

"What?"

"She likes oatmeal, and that won't be too rough on her stomach."

"Oh, okay. I'll pick her up some oatmeal," he says, giving me a look that I don't try to decipher.

Heath and Chris wave as they leave, and I sit back in the chair beside her bed.

Chapter Twenty-Three

KIM

When I open my eyes, the sunlight is spilling into the room. Declan is sitting in the chair beside my bed, where he always is when I wake up.

"Good morning beautiful, how do you feel today?"

"I feel okay. Not so groggy, thank goodness," I tell him.

I try to sit up, and he immediately gets up to help me adjust the bed and pillows.

"Thank you," I tell him as I look up into his eyes.

I can see the heat and desire in them, and it sends shivers down my body, making my pussy clench with need.

Damn, it's been a long time since I've felt him inside me. Of course, I would think that too if it had only been two hours. I lick my lips as the dirty thoughts race through my mind. Just as he leans down to kiss my lips, the door to the room opens, and I whisper, "Bathroom."

"Kimmy," Heath starts to say but then stops.

Declan nods and helps me by grabbing the IV pole and helping me off the bed.

"Hey sweetie, sorry, have to go to the bathroom," I tell him as I shuffle past him.

"Don't forget to brush that mouth," he calls out, then mutters, "I don't know what you've been doing with it."

But I hear him as I close the door to the bathroom. I let out a slow breath, my pussy wet with need. "Damn, Heath," I mutter.

I use the toilet, wash my hands, then brush my teeth before going back out into the room. I notice Declan is already gone, but Heath is there with a bowl of something.

"What's in the bowl?" I ask as I push the IV pole and walk toward the bed.

"Oatmeal," he says.

"Oh, I love oatmeal," I tell him, beaming.

"So I was told," he says nonchalantly.

"Huh?"

"Oh, nothing, come on, get in the bed, and we can eat," he tells me, helping to put the IV pole back where it goes, and helping me get back on the bed.

Once I'm covered, he puts the tray in front of me with the bowl of oatmeal and a spoon. I take the first bite and moan as the flavors hit my tongue.

"Oh, wow, this is really good. What is it?"

"I don't know, but I'm glad you like it. It's the house oatmeal from the cute little diner by my place."

"It really is good," I tell him while taking another bite.

We continue eating in silence, and I occasionally catch Heath watching me.

"Okay, what gives?" I ask.

"Whaaatt?" he tries to act surprised by my question.

"You have been sneaking looks at me, not talking, what is going on?"

"I just want you to be able to eat with some peace and quiet. I know you had a rough day yesterday with the whole heart thing, so this is me just making sure you are okay," he tells me, going back to his breakfast sandwich.

"Oh?" I say, looking back down at my oatmeal, feeling awkwardly silly now.

"Well, there is something else I want to ask," he starts to say, but the phone in the room rings, and my heart starts to beat frantically.

I look up at Heath and see the fear in his eyes as well.

He walks over to the phone, **"Hello?"** he asks as he answers.

I watch his shoulders deflate, and he says, **"Oh no, honey, they must have hit a couple of wrong numbers."**

"A huh."

"Okay, have a good day," then he hangs up.

I look at him quizzically.

"Seems the receptionist dialed the wrong room number, no worries."

I nod, but my heart is still beating, and I can't stomach another bite.

"Are you done?" Heath asks, frowning.

"Yeah, I can't eat anymore," I tell him, feeling anxious, even though I know I don't need to be.

Heath said it was a wrong number, and I'm sure it probably was, but all of a sudden, I hear the man's voice again, this time a little distorted. A memory forms in my mind.

"Kimberly...it's time to wake up," he says as he slaps my face.

I open my eyes, and he laughs. I can't see his face, but I can hear him. My arms are above my head, handcuffed to something above me. I can't make out what it is since the light in here is very dim.

I'm still wearing my running outfit, leggings, and sports bra. My shoes and socks are no longer on me, so he must have taken them off.

"Are you ready to play my game, Kimberly?" he whispers in my ear.

I jump because I didn't know he was behind me, and he laughs, walking away a short distance.

He makes no sound with his feet. I can't tell how far away he is right now.

"Oh, you are going to be so fun to break, Kimberly."

Okay, he's a little distance behind me, I think as I close my eyes and focus on my other senses.

There's an odor of disinfectant, not strong and overpowering, but definitely enough to know some cleaning had been done.

There is a stale dampness in the air. I must be in a basement or something like it.

I hear chains moving, but I know they aren't mine as I'm hanging here and not moving.

"Oh, Kimberly, you've been a bad girl," he says before I feel the first punch to my gut.

It knocks the breath out of me as I was not expecting it.

"You hung up on me," he says, sounding pissed before he hits me again.

"You ignored my calls," and I realize he's getting angrier.

The angrier his voice, the harder his hits become.

Soon, my body and face hurt. I don't know how many times he hit me. I felt like a punching bag as he continues to deliver blow after blow.

Finally, he stops, but he doesn't leave. I hear chains move and then a wrenching scream before I hear the grunts of a man and the squeaking of rusty springs.

Oh my God, he's raping someone, I think to myself, but I can't see anything through my swollen eyes. I think the bastard broke my jaw. I can't open my mouth to say anything.

When he finishes, he stands up, and he's back in front of me. I can smell his breath, and he says, "Your FBI friends will never find you. You are mine for as long as I want to play the game, but make no mistakes, Kimberly, I will break you, like I break them all."

He laughs and leaves the room, but not before I feel a prick in my arm.

What the hell? I think before things go weird in my mind.

"Kimmy, earth to Kimmy," I hear Heath say, and I blink back in focus. "Hey, where were you just then?" he asks, giving me a worried look.

"I remember," I whisper.

"You remember what?" he asks.

"I remember waking up to a slap across my face and him telling me to wake up. I remember him beating my body like I was a punching bag, and, Heath, I think he raped another female," I tell him.

"Oh my God, Kimmy, he has another victim?"

I nod my head.

"Do you know where you were?"

I shake my head. "No, but I think it was a basement or something below ground. There was a stale dampness, but I could also smell cleaner."

"Cleaner?" he questions, and I can only nod as I try to remember more.

"I need to call Eric and let him know what to look for in their search this morning," he says, pulling his phone out.

"Search?" I ask.

"Yeah, some abandoned buildings they found when they followed your footprints in the woods before the rain washed them away, that is. **Oh, hey, Eric. Yeah, Kim remembered something.**"

"Yeah, she's right here, hold on," he says, handing me the phone.

"Hey, Eric," I say before I tell him what I remembered.

"Okay, thanks, Kim. We will look for any areas that may resemble that," he tells me before hanging up.

"I'm so sorry you went through that, babe," Heath tells me, putting the phone back in his pocket.

I want to change the subject, so I say, "Tell me about Boston."

"Oh girl, well we started off searching for you. Declan and I went to your place..."

"My place?" I ask, interrupting him.

"Yeah. That's the last place you were at."

"How do you know?" I ask.

"Your car was in the driveway, your purse and keys were in the house on your console. The only thing missing was your phone, and it was turned off, so we couldn't even locate you," he tells me. "Plus, Declan told us he was there to pick you up for dinner."

"He told you that?" I ask, but I guess he would have to tell them that in order to know I was missing.

"Yes. Do you not remember any of that?" he asks.

"Sort of. I vaguely remember Declan calling and me telling him all the things that still needed to be done for Michelle and Eric's wedding. He said he'd pick me up for dinner, and we could go through the list together," I tell him, not bothering to mention our relationship.

"Oh," Heath says, sounding disappointed.

"Why do you sound disappointed?" I ask.

"I thought maybe there was something more there. Maybe it's one-sided," he says thoughtfully.

"What are you talking about?" I ask.

"Nothing, so anyways, back to my story. Eric got a call that there was a potential serial killer murdering on trains that left Largo and made a stop in Boston. So he assigned Mya and myself to go check it out."

"Well, I'm assuming it was a serial killer, but on a Train? How?"

"Let me finish, sugar, because when you hear who the killer turned out to be, you are going to flip," he says as he tells me everything.

"Wow, and you didn't know?" I ask, finding it unbelievable.

"Not an ounce, until I was literally hit over the head and shackled in a barn stall. A barn stall," he says dramatically as he puts his hand over his heart like that is the worst thing in the world.

"At least it was only a few hours, and you were passed out for it," I tell him, melancholy in my voice.

"True," he replies with a sadness in his tone.

"But, hey, you found Rayeanne, so you closed two cases in one shot," I say, trying to bring his mood back up. There is nothing worse than a sad Heath.

"Yep. Can you believe she was being held that whole time, all because she accidentally walked in on the killer," he says, shaking his head.

"At least she is back with her family. I know Detective Burton must be thrilled to have her back and to know it wasn't a family member who did anything."

"Right," he says before adding, "I'm just glad everything worked out. I may have gotten a concussion for it all, but it was still a happy ending, and look, you've had me to talk with during the days. I can't imagine Declan is much of a talker during your night shifts."

"Why do you say that?" I ask, genuinely interested in his response.

"Because girlie, every time I come in here with food, you are asleep," he says dramatically.

I can't help the laugh that escapes me.

"He really isn't boring. If anyone is boring, it has to be me. I fall asleep, and he has no one to talk to," I tell him, feeling bad now that I have said that out loud.

I think Heath understands my expression because he says, "I'm sure he would rather you rest, and he sit in silence, than to have you worn out and it be all his fault."

"I'm sure you are right," I say with a smile.

I decide to make it up to him tonight. Show him my appreciation that I know he will enjoy, and so will I. I can't help the giddiness that overcomes me with my thoughts. I may not have chocolate or ice cubes, but I will still make it special for him.

Heath and I spend the rest of the morning doing some light yoga stretches and walks before the nurse comes in with the next dose of antibiotics for the fluid in my heart. I really hope this cures everything. I am ready to go home.

After the nurse administers the antibiotic, my room phone rings. Heath and I both look at each other.

"Want me to get it again?" he asks, but I shake my head.

"No. I need to do this," I tell him, reaching over and picking up the receiver.

"Hello," I state, sounding more confident than what I really feel.

Heath walks up next to me, and I tilt the phone so we both can hear.

"Kim...ber...ly," he sings my name in a sweet, sickly voice.

"What do you want?" I ask, allowing the anger to rise today.

"**Oh, someone has remembered something, hasn't she?**" he laughs.

I don't say anything, and he sings my name again. I watch Heath as he shutters.

"**Kim...ber..ly, it's almost time to come back and play.**"

"**Why won't you leave me alone,**" I say, through gritted teeth.

"**Because you are not broken yet, but you will be very soon,**" he says before he hangs up.

I stare at the phone in my shaking hands, before Heath takes it and puts it on the cradle.

"Girl, that man is crazy, but don't you worry, he can't get to you. The team and I will never allow it to happen," he tells me, but I can't shake the feeling in the pit of my stomach that they won't be able to stop him.

Chapter Twenty-Four

DECLAN

I call Eric on my way to the hospital to see how the search went or is going.

"Declan," he answers.

"Hey, boss, any updates?" I ask.

"Where are you?"

"Driving to the hospital, but I wanted to check in before I got there?" I tell him.

"We are checking on a lead that Kim gave us," he tells me, and I can't hide the shock in my voice.

"Kim?" I ask.

"Yeah. She remembered something about where she was held. You'll have to ask her about it when you get there. We are still searching," he tells me as the phone starts to break up.

"Okay, Boss. Let me know if you find anything."

"Will do," he says, then hangs up.

I can't help but wonder what Kim remembered and why didn't she call me. "Well, duh, you stupid idiot, it's because Heath is there," I chastise myself.

God, days like this, I hate that our relationship is being kept a secret from the rest of the team.

I rub my face with my hand, knowing I need to get my shit together. This isn't about me, it's about Kim and keeping her safe.

I get to Kim's room, and I find her sleeping and Heath reading a book. He looks up when I open the door and says, "Hey."

"Hey. How long has she been sleeping?" I ask him quietly.

"As soon as the antibiotic kicked in, but after the phone call," he tells me.

"Phone call?" I ask.

"Yeah, creepy man called her."

"You let her answer the phone?" I ask through gritted teeth, pissed off.

"She wanted to do it since she remembered some things, which weren't pretty, by the way," he says with a disgusted look on his face.

"What did she remember?" I ask, not wanting to know but needing to.

"She remembers being handcuffed above her head and used like a punching bag. She thinks she was in a basement or something close to it, and she's pretty sure there was another female there whom the man raped," he tells me as he shivers.

"Does she remember how she got free?"

"No," he says with a sigh, "But what she did remember is enough to scar anyone."

"Did she ever see his face?"

He shakes his head. "She said the light was very dim."

"What did he say on the phone?"

"His voice was a little distorted, like he was using something to cover his true voice, but pretty much told her he was coming for her. I told her not to worry about it, because we would never let that happen," he says, though I can hear the doubt in his voice.

"You are right, we will never let that happen. The sooner we can get her out of this hospital, the better," I tell him, but it was more for me.

I'll be damned if this mad man, whoever the hell he is, takes my woman again. I can't lose her again. I don't think I would survive it this time, I internally tell myself.

"Right. Did you bring food?" Heath asks.

"Damn," I say, shaking my head. "I was going to stop and pick up something, but I forgot after my phone conversation with Eric," I tell him, looking sheepishly.

"You talked to Eric?" he asks.

"Yeah. I wanted to see how the search was going, and he informed me they were looking into a lead that Kim remembered something about," I tell him, looking back at the bed where Kim is still sleeping.

"Oh. Well, I hope they find something."

"Me too, but hey, if you don't mind staying a little while longer, I'll run out and get some food."

"No worries, I'll pick something up for you both and bring it back. Chris is working late tonight, so I don't have any plans. We can all eat together again," he says, then frowns.

"What is it?" I ask.

"She hasn't been eating much. I'm worried she's going to lose too much weight."

"I'm sure the antibiotics don't help, but don't forget, her stomach probably shrank a lot. I don't think that man fed her anything, and then she was in a coma for over six weeks. It will take time. Anything we can get in her at this point is a win," I tell him.

He looks thoughtful before he says, "You're right. Everything takes time. I'll be back." Then he walks out the door.

I sit in the seat next to Kim's bed and wait for her to wake up and Heath to bring the food back, as my mind replays the conversation with Heath about the phone call.

Can we keep her safe? My mind says yes, but my gut tells me no, and I will lose her again. *"No,"* I tell myself, shaking my head. *"I will not lose her again. I will make sure she stays safe."*

It's not long until Heath returns with some food, and Kim rouses from her sleep.

"Hey," she says when she sees me.

"Hey. Are you ready to eat?" I ask as Heath unpacks the bag.

"Yeah, but do you have anything light in there? I don't think I can handle anything heavy today," she says, and I frown.

"Why?" Heath and I both ask.

"I think the antibiotics are suppressing my appetite, and even though I know I need to eat, my stomach is telling a different story," she says, sighing.

"I did pick you up some soup and bread," Heath says, passing me the bowl of soup.

I get up from the chair and grab her table before placing it in front of her. I set down the soup and Heath passes her a spoon and some bread from the restaurant.

"Thank you, guys," she says with a smile and then a yawn escapes her.

Heath pulls up the other chair, and we both watch as she spoons some soup into her mouth.

"Oh, wow, this is really good. Chicken noodle?" she asks.

"I think so," Heath tells her.

Thankfully she eats the whole bowl and half a piece of bread.

I watch as she yawns, then looks at us. "I'm sorry guys, but I can't seem to keep my eyes open anymore," she says, slurring her words as her eyes close.

"It's fine. Sleep," Heath tells her. "At least she ate more than she normally does," he whispers to me, and I nod my head.

I grab her tray, move it to the side, and bag up all the empty containers. Heath takes them and says, "I'll see you in the morning."

I nod as I take a seat back in the chair I vacated.

A week later

"Alright, Ms. Santiago, let's see if the antibiotics worked," Doctor Spencer says as they take Kim back down to radiology to do another echocardiogram to check on the fluid.

I wait in the room where I was last time, with the wheelchair and her clothes.

The past few days, she seems to be doing better. She's walking around more, not sleeping as much, even with getting the dose of antibiotics. Her appetite has grown, and she looks to be putting some weight back on.

The nurse brings her back into the room, and I help her get her clothes back on before wheeling her back upstairs. Once I get her back in the bed, Doctor Spenser comes in with Doctor Sava.

"Great news, Doctor Spencer starts, "The fluid around your heart is gone, so I will want to see you back in six months to make sure it doesn't come back. Should you feel like something is off before then, don't hesitate to call me, and we will check it," he says.

"Sounds good, Doctor, thank you," she says with a smile.

Doctor Spencer leaves, and Doctor Sava looks at us both. "Now that there is no danger to your heart and you've met the other criteria, we are going to release you," he tells Kim with a smile.

"Really?" she asks.

"Really. All your blood work has come back normal. You are able to walk and eat, so I see no reason to keep you any longer. I'll have the nurse come in and take your IV out while I sign your discharge papers, and then you will be free to leave."

"Thank you, Doctor Sava," she says happily, looking over at me, and I can't keep the grin off my face.

I send Eric a text letting him know the good news.

Doctor Sava leaves the room, and Kim shrieks with excitement. "Oh my God, I never thought this day would ever come," she says.

"It's about time for sure," I tell her with a smile. "I'm looking forward to having you in my arms all night," I add, and I watch her eyes dilate with the implications of my words.

"I am too," she says huskily as she licks her lips.

Just then, the nurse comes in to take out the IV while I pack up all her stuff. I think Heath brought half her closet to the hospital. I silently decide, whatever I am unable to stuff in her bag, I'll just carry as I shake my head.

Once the nurse is done taking Kim's IV out, and I have all her belongings organized, the nurse goes to get a wheelchair to wheel Kim out of the hospital.

"Why do I need to get in the wheelchair." Kim stomps her foot. "I just want the papers and to go."

"It's hospital policy, you know that," I tell her softly. "Also, if you don't do it, they won't release you," I add, and those words seem to change her attitude.

The nurse comes in with the wheelchair, as another nurse brings in a bouquet of flowers.

"Oh, who are those for?" Kim asks before sitting down in the chair.

"They are for you, dear, they were just delivered," the nurse pushing the wheelchair says.

"Oh, how sweet. I wonder who sent them," she says as she sits in the chair and takes the flowers. "They are beautiful," she gushes, and I kick myself for never bringing her flowers.

"This was also delivered," the other nurse who brought in the flowers said as she hands Kim a small box.

"Wow, thank you," she says with a smile as she places the box on her lap and takes the card from the flowers to read it.

I watch as the smile on her face falls.

"What's wrong?" I ask, and she hands me the card.

KIMBERLY

I CAN'T WAIT TO HAVE YOU BACK WHERE YOU BELONG

There is no signature, not that I really expected to see one with those words. I reach over and take the box from her lap. I open it up, and find a cell phone.

"What the hell?" I mutter.

I close the box back up, knowing I will have Eric give this to the Cyber team to find out if there is anything on it.

I take the flowers from Kim and follow her and the nurse out of the room. Before we get to the elevator, I throw the flowers in the nearest garbage can. No way will I allow those things in her house. If she wants flowers, I will buy her some flowers.

I leave the nurse and Kim at the front of the building while I get the car. When I pull up, it takes no time to get Kim settled in the front seat. We wave goodbye to the nurse, and I drive away.

"Let's get you home," I tell her as I lay my hand on her thigh, squeezing a little bit.

"Yes, finally, let's go home," she answers, but no longer sounding excited.

Chapter Twenty-Five

KIM

Declan is driving us to my house, and though I'm excited to be out of the hospital, I can't quell the feeling that something bad is going to happen.

He sent me flowers. I should have known not to get excited. Not once since my stay in the hospital did any of my friends bring me flowers. I internally chastise myself. He sent me a cell phone. Why did he send me a cell phone, when he knew my room number? He can't know that I'm being discharged.

"Why the cell phone?" I say out loud.

"What do you mean?" Declan asks.

"Why did he send me a cell phone? He knew my room number. He called the hospital room at least twice. Why did he send me a cell phone with the flowers?"

"You think he knows you were discharged?" he asks thoughtfully.

"But how could he? The decision was just made. You only told Eric, right?"

"Yeah, I sent him a text," Declan says, mulling over my questions.

We both spend the rest of the drive in silence, lost in our thoughts.

I barely notice when we pull up to my house until I hear Declan say, "What have they done?"

"What?" I ask, looking over at him before I look out at the front of my house.

There is a big banner that says, WELCOME HOME!!, and the smiling faces of Michelle, Eric, Mya, Heath, and Frankie.

"Wow, the gang's all here," I say softly, touched by the warm homecoming.

Declan pulls to a stop in my driveway and Michelle is the first one at my door. I step out of the car, and she pulls me in for a hug.

"I'm so glad you are finally home," she whispers in my ear.

When she pulls back, I see the tears pooling in her eyes, and judging by the big smile on her face, I know she is really happy.

Heath is the next one to give me a hug, followed by Mya, then Frankie, and finally Eric.

"Not that I'm not happy to see you all, but what are you doing here?" I ask, giving them a smile so they know I don't mean it in a derogatory way.

"We wanted to be the first to welcome you home," Shelly says. "Come on, I made us some dinner."

She wraps her arm around mine and leads me into the house. *So much for a quiet night at home,* I think to myself, but keep the smile on my face.

I see Declan pull Eric to the side as we walk by, and I know he will be telling him about the cell phone and flowers.

We walk into the house, and I smell something that makes my mouth water. Shelly leads me into my kitchen, and there on the island is a spread of food, enough to feed an army. She really outdid herself.

I take a look at everything that is laid out, and there is a pot roast, salad, rolls, mashed potatoes, gravy, corn on the cob, pizza, lasagna, garlic bread, "Damn, woman, I think you went overboard," I tell her.

"I told you," Eric says as he comes up behind her, kissing her on the top of her head.

"Well, I wasn't sure what you would want, so I got everything that I knew you would eat," she says, biting her lip.

"How many other people are coming?" I ask.

"Just us," she says, looking at me questioningly.

"Woman, there is enough food here to feed an army," I tell her, laughing.

"Some of this will be leftovers, so you don't have to cook for a couple of days," she tells me as she starts to relax. "Now, fix you a plate."

I take the plate from Shelly, putting a little pot roast, salad, potatoes, and corn on the cob on the plate. I make my way over to the dining table and take a seat as everyone else fills their plates up.

Once everyone is seated, we dig in, laughing, telling stories, and eating. I can feel myself beginning to relax since we left the hospital.

I look around the table at everyone, and I can't lie, it feels good to be home. We feel like a team again, even if it's not what I expected. I am happy to see everyone here and to know I'm no longer in the hospital.

After we eat, Heath and Mya bring out a cake, and I don't know how they think I'm supposed to eat anything else.

"We can't have a celebration without a cake," Heath says as I narrow my eyes at this cake.

"Where am I supposed to put it?" I ask.

"In your mouth, unless you want to wear it, and then that's on you," he says, waving his hand.

Everyone laughs, and I can only shake my head.

"I just mean, I can't eat another bite of anything," I tell him with a smile on my face.

"As my dear mama would say, 'You're too skinny, we need to put meat on them bones, eat...eat'," he says in the accent of an Italian woman.

I eye him warily, "I didn't realize your mother was Italian?"

"She likes to think she is, but regardless, that didn't stop her from acting like one," Heath says sheepishly, and we all laugh.

I take a small piece of cake, so as not to hurt anyone, including dear mama's feelings.

By the time we are done, I feel like I'm going to explode from the amount of food I have eaten. I'm still not used to eating so much.

"When should we start running again?" Heath asks, patting his stomach.

"How about tomorrow?" I say as I rub mine to ease the ache, "Though I think we will have to start off slow."

"Sounds good to me. Shelly?" Heath asks, and she looks over at me with concern.

"Are you sure you want to run so soon after getting out of the hospital?"

"Yes, I'm sure. I laid around for too long in that bed, plus the doctor said I could resume my activities," I tell her.

"What about your heart?"

"It's fine, or at least it was before I ate all this food," I say with a laugh, and that loosens everyone else up, and they laugh with me.

"Touche," Shelly says, smiling, "Okay, we start back tomorrow."

With that settled, everyone picks up their dishes and heads to the kitchen.

"Just leave everything in the sink, I will get it," I tell them all.

"We can help clean up," Shelly says, but I shake my head.

"No, I got this. You all did so much already for me. You don't need to clean my kitchen. I got this, and I promise it won't take me all night to do," I tell her with a laugh.

"Are you sure?"

"Yes, I'm sure. You all should go home, I'm sure you're exhausted, but thank you for the welcome home dinner and cake. It was wonderful," I tell them.

Shelly gives me a hug. "As long as you are sure," she says.

I laugh. "I'm sure."

Mya is the next to give me a hug and whispers, "I'm glad your home."

"Thank you," I whisper back, "Oh and I want to hear all about Shane."

I watch as she blushes, but she gives me a nod.

Heath gives me a hug, "Will you be in the office tomorrow?"

Before I can answer, Eric calls out, "No, she will need a few days to adjust to not being in the hospital."

"Actually, boss, if you don't mind, I would like to come back to work tomorrow. The sooner I can get back into the groove, the better," I tell him confidently.

He looks at me and then nods. "Okay, we will see you in the morning then."

I smile at his approval. "Yay," I say, and everyone laughs. "Thank you, guys, again for everything.".

"See you in the morning, buttercup," Heath says as he walks toward the door.

"I'm glad you are home," Frankie says, hugging me.

I can't help but tense up at his touch, but I pull back and give him a small smile. "See you all in the morning," I say, and he nods, following Heath toward the door.

"See you all in the morning," Mya tells me with a wave, as she too, heads for the door.

"Are you sure I can't help you clean up?" Shelly asks.

"No," I say with a laugh. "Declan and I will get this. Go home with your husband and relax. I'll see you tomorrow," I tell her.

"You don't have to tell me twice, come on, woman," Eric says, trying to push Shelly toward the door.

"Okay, okay," she says, with her own laugh, and gives me another hug. "I'll see you tomorrow."

"Five o'clock," I call back, and she gives me a wave over her shoulder before closing the front door.

I walk over and lock it, taking a deep breath and sighing. I walk back to the kitchen, and Declan is putting the food away, so I start loading the dishwasher.

"I got this, babe, why don't you go soak in a hot bath. You haven't been able to do that in a while," Declan tells me, and I like that idea a lot.

"Are you sure? I would feel slightly guilty for leaving you to clean up this mess," I tease.

"Slightly?" he says, quirking an eyebrow up.

I giggle and say, "Yes, slightly because a hot bath sounds wonderful right now."

He leans down and gives me a kiss, then says with a smile, "Go, take your bath. I've got this."

I don't wait for him to change his mind. I quickly make a beeline for my bathroom. I immediately start the water, waiting for the perfect temperature, before I leave it to fill. When it's halfway full, I add in my lavender bubble bath, strip out of my clothes, and sink into the hot water.

"God, this feels like heaven," I say aloud as I slide down until the hot water is below my neck.

I lay there soaking, enjoying the heat as it soaks into my bones and melding into my muscles. I can feel them relaxing as the tension seeps out. I don't know how long I lay in there, but the water begins to go cold, and I know it's time for me to get out.

I feel more relaxed than I have in, I don't know how long. Definitely in the last eight weeks, that's for sure. I grab a towel and begin to dry off, but Declan takes the towel from me, and without saying anything, begins to slowly dry my body.

He starts with my left leg, patting the towel up my leg slowly and stopping at my upper thigh before moving over to my right leg and doing the same as the other one.

I can feel the heat of his breath on my vagina, and my core clenches with need.

"Did you enjoy your bath?" he asks in a whisper as the heat of his breath causes my skin to pebble, and a moan escapes me.

He takes the towel up the back of my legs, patting my ass before he squeezes with both hands. His face is really close to my pussy, but he's not touching me where I need him to.

"How are you doing?" he asks in a sultry whisper.

"Frustrated," I admit as I lean my head back.

"Oh, how can I fix that for you?"

"Touch me," I beg him.

"I am touching you," he chuckles and continues moving the towel up my back.

His face is now at my stomach, the heat from his breath has mine hitching.

"Please, Declan," I beg him.

Chapter Twenty-Six

DECLAN

I chuckle as she begs me to touch her. I love how I am able to tease her, without really doing anything. I only wanted to dry her off, but being so close to her body, smelling the lavender, feeling her heat, I couldn't help myself.

My cock is painfully hard, and I want to take her right here, but I know she needs more before we get to that point, and I am here to show her just that. To her, I may be teasing, but for me, I am waking her up and showing her how much I love her.

I stand up, looking down at her before I move to her back and place the towel to her front. I start patting her dry from her stomach, and I work my way up, paying very close attention to her breasts with the towel.

"Declan, you are killing me," she says as she leans her head back onto my chest.

"Are you not enjoying being pampered?" I ask her.

"Are you pampering me, or teasing me?" she asks as her breathing picks up.

"I am," I say, not committing to one or the other.

I lean down and pepper her neck with small kisses.

"Mmmm," she moans.

She moves her hand to her back and starts rubbing my cock through my pants. "Woman, I'm supposed to be pampering you," I grit out.

"Oh, was that what you were doing?" Her breaths get heavy as she juts out her breasts while rubbing my cock.

"Fuck this," I say as I drop the towel and squeeze her breasts.

"Yes," she moans out.

I turn her around and kiss her lips. She opens her mouth for me, and I take full advantage of it. Slipping my tongue into her mouth while enjoying the feel and taste of her. Our tongues battle and everything turns heated quickly.

I grab her ass and lift her up. She immediately wraps her legs around me and begins rubbing her pussy against my hard cock.

I take her to the bedroom and lay her on the bed, never breaking our kiss. I explore her body with my hand before following it with my lips. I need to get reacquainted with her body. It's been too long.

I kiss down her body until my face is settled between her thighs, and I'm breathing in her aroma. I can see how wet she is with her pussy glistening.

I swipe my tongue up through her folds, moaning from her taste. It's been too long, and I can't help myself as I thrust my tongue inside her, tasting her juices. I suck and lick her clit, causing her to bow her back from the pleasure I am giving her.

"OH, GOD, Declan, so good," she calls out.

I flick her clit with my tongue before sucking it into my mouth while I insert a finger inside her, building her up. She's rocking her hips, holding my head, as she fucks my face, and I don't mind one bit.

I breathe onto her clit, before I suck it back into my mouth as I add another finger inside her to help stretch her and get her ready for me. I can feel her walls starting to contract and pulse. I know she's close, and I pick up the pace as I fuck her with my fingers.

"So close," she moans out, and I keep going. "Please, Declan," she says.

I bite down on her clit, not too hard, but hard enough for her to explode. I replace my fingers with my tongue, wanting to lap up her juices.

I look up at her from where I am, and I can see the ecstasy she's exuding through the glow of her skin.

I stand up, take my pants off, and my shirt, leaving them on the floor. I climb back on the bed to get between her legs, needing to feel her pussy wrapped around my cock. I line myself up at her entrance and then slowly thrust inside her, taking my time before I'm completely seated inside her.

"Oh my," she whispers as she wraps her legs around my waist and thrusts up to meet me.

"You are so beautiful, and you feel amazing," I tell her before kissing her lips.

"You feel so good too, God, it's been too long," she tells me as her fingers dig into my shoulders.

"Oh, oh," she moans out as the sound of our skin slapping together fills the room.

"Oh, Kim," I groan out.

Being with her is the highlight of my life, and I want her to know how much I love her as I continue to thrust into her, showing her with my body, how much she means to me.

"Declan, I'm so close," she tells me, and I pick up the pace, thrusting harder and deeper.

"Yes, yes, more, Declan. Oh God, yes, just like that," she tells me before her orgasm detonates with her juices coating my cock, allowing me to get deeper inside her. I can feel my spine tingling and my balls tighten before I unload my cum deep inside her. I groan her name as I come.

We both lie there, catching our breaths and getting our bearings back. Once I can feel my body again, I pull out slowly and roll to the other side of her.

"Wow, that was..." she starts.

"Perfect," I finish, because it was perfect.

"Yes, it was," she says, cuddling up to me on my chest.

It only takes us both minutes before we succumb to sleep in each other's arms.

I'm pulled from my slumber, and at first, I'm not sure what it was that woke me, until I feel her mouth on me and hear her slurping as she goes down on me. She's working my cock like it's her own lollipop, and I lay here enjoying the feel of her mouth wrapped around me, that is until she gags when my cock hits the back of her throat as she takes me deep.

I try to give her this time, but I'm lost in the feel and ecstasy of her mouth, that I place my hands on her head and thrust up at the same time.

I feel her moan more than I hear it, and it sends vibrations through me that have my hips moving up faster.

"Oh, fuck, babe, your mouth feels amazing," I moan out as I continue to thrust into her mouth.

I can feel my balls tighten up, and she continues to suck and deep throat me, and the minute she starts to massage them, I lose it and come into her mouth. She sucks me clean and doesn't stop until I'm semi-hard again.

"Fuck babe, now that was a wake-up call," I tell her when she finally comes out of the covers, and I can see her face.

She licks her lips and gives me a smile. "I've wanted to do that since the hospital, but those damn antibiotics kept knocking me out," she admits, and I can't help but pull her in for a kiss.

"My turn," I tell her as I kiss down her body, all the way to her pussy. As soon as my tongue swipes between her folds, tasting how wet she is, she bucks off the bed.

I place my hand on her stomach, holding her down as I feast on her swollen, wet pussy.

"Oh, God, Declan, please, I need more," she calls out.

I trade my tongue out for my fingers, making sure to curl them at the right angle to hit her sweet spot while I suck and flick on her clit. I feel her walls tighten around my fingers.

"Oh yes, Declan, yes," she moans out, and I don't stop.

I replace my fingers with my mouth again, and she places her fingers through my hair, pulling and pushing as she thrusts her hips up and rubs her pussy on my mouth.

I look up to her face, and she has her head thrown back and the other hand-on her breast, pinching her nipple.

She looks so damn erotic right now, and I can't help the hard on that is currently pressing into the bed as my mouth continues to assault her pussy, and my finger plays with her clit, waiting for her to come in my mouth.

She doesn't keep me waiting long as her body tightens up before her orgasm explodes, she screams out my name, and I love hearing it from her lips.

"Declan, oh God, Declan, yes."

I lick and suck all her juices before climbing up her body and thrusting my cock inside her.

"Oh, damn, baby. You feel so fucking good," I tell her when I'm all the way inside her.

I kiss her lips, allowing her to taste herself on me as I slowly move inside her, savoring the feel of her tight pussy wrapped around me.

Neither of us say anything as we meet each other's thrusts, our bodies coated in sweat as they rub against each other.

It doesn't take long for us both to come and this time, we come together, calling out each other's names.

When we come back down from our orgasmic bliss and our breathing is manageable, I look her in the eyes and tell her, "I love you, always and forever."

She gives me her perfect smile and says, "I love you, always and forever."

I give her one more kiss before looking at the clock. "We have an hour to get ready for work. Why don't you jump in the shower first, and I'll go make the coffee."

"Sounds good to me, but you could join me," she says seductively.

I shake my head, "No, woman. If I do that, we will never get to work."

She laughs as she gets out of bed and heads to the bathroom. "Oh, we will make it to work, we just may be a few hours late."

"You are going to be the death of me, woman," I mutter, making my way to the kitchen to make the coffee.

Chapter Twenty-Seven

KIM

I can't help the smile I currently have on my face. Declan did get in the shower with me after he made the coffee, so we are only running twenty minutes behind. I almost forgot my running clothes and had to quickly pack my bag.

Now, I'm walking up the sidewalk to our office building, Declan already having gone in first, since we are both late, I thought it best if I was a little later than him.

When I get off the elevator and walk into the office area, I notice everything still looks the same. Nothing has changed, and for that, I am grateful.

"Hey, Kim, are you okay?" Mya asks.

"Yeah, I'm just running behind today. I would have been here on time, but I had to run back to the house after forgetting my running clothes for this afternoon."

She nods in understanding, then says, "Eric wants to see you as soon as you get in."

"Okay, thanks," I tell her, dropping my stuff off at my desk and walking to Eric's office.

I knock on his door. "Hey, boss, you wanted to see me?"

"Yeah, how are you feeling today?" he asks as he stands up from his desk and walks around it.

"I'm good. I guess it will take me a few days to get back into the old rhythm, but I'll get there. I'm sorry I'm a little late," I tell him.

He waves his hand to bat the thought away. "No worries. I'm going to take Declan, Heath, and Mya with me to look at some areas. Frankie will be here with you, are you good with that?" he asks.

Am I good with that? I don't know. I mean, Frankie has never done anything except annoy me like a little brother, but I also know he wants more than that status, I've been able to keep him at bay, so this shouldn't be an issue either. "Yeah, boss, I'm good with that," I tell him, giving him a small smile.

"Okay, good. Now, here is a phone," he starts as he passes me a cell phone.

I look at him curiously, hoping it's not the phone that the madman sent me.

"No, it's not that phone. I'm having the techs go through that phone to see if there is anything useful. No, this is a new company phone that you can use. The only numbers in there are Michelle's, mine, and Declan's. I don't know how the man has gotten your numbers, and for safety reasons, I don't want anyone besides us four to know you have a phone."

"Okay, boss," I tell him as I place the phone in my pocket.

"If at any point today, you feel overwhelmed, do not hesitate to go home," he tells me pointedly.

I can't help the laugh that escapes me. "You know that will not happen, but sure, if I get overwhelmed, I'll go home."

He also laughs because he does know me. He knows no matter what, I will stick it out. "Okay, fine, have it your way, just make sure to take care of yourself."

"I will, and Eric, thank you," I say before leaving his office.

I know he cares about us all. That's just the type of boss he is. I go back to my cubicle, boot up my computer, and see what the day has in store for me.

When I open my emails, I see I'm in for a long day. I currently have over seventeen hundred in my inbox.

"Fuck," I mutter.

"What's wrong, Kimmy?" Heath asks as he comes up behind me.

"I'm going to be drowning in emails for the rest of the month," I tell him, giving him a pout.

"Girl, you got this, you are the queen of emails," he tells me laughing, and he isn't wrong. I know I'll have half of this replied to before lunch, but that's not the point.

"Heath, Declan, Mya, you are with me today," Eric says when he comes out of his office.

"What about me, Boss?" Frankie asks.

"I want you to stay here with Kim today and try to track down those burner phones. I want to know where they came from," Eric tells him, and Frankie nods, giving me his most blinding smile.

"Okay, Boss, no problem," he says as he sits back down at his desk.

Eric nods at me, and then he and the rest of the team leave. I get busy with these emails.

I don't realize how much time has passed until Frankie walks up to my desk and says, "Hey, we have to go."

I jump because I never heard him move from his desk.

"Go? Go where?" I ask him.

"I'm not sure. Eric just texted me and said he needs us both at their location."

"Why didn't he call me?" I wonder out loud.

"Probably because you don't have a phone yet," he responds.

"Oh yeah," I say, forgetting that Frankie is not aware of the cell phone in my pocket.

"Let's go. I'll drive," he tells me, and I grab my jacket off the back of my chair.

We get in the government vehicle, and he puts the address in the GPS before putting the car in drive.

We drive out of the city of Largo, and I see woods all around us. My mind gets pulled into a memory.

There is something wrong with that face, I tell myself. It can't be real. I close my eyes, blinking several times, and when I open my eyes again, it's gone, but I can hear the laugh as it moves away. It sounds manic and gleeful at the same time.

I need to get out of here, but how? I've been put in a chair, and my hands are handcuffed to this pole. Think Kim, think.

I try to look around, my eyes are so swollen I can't see anything. I move my hands to feel along the pole, ahh, there. I found a small nail sticking out. I manage to get the nail into the keyhole on the handcuffs. It takes me a few maneuvers, but I finally get one side unlocked, then I get the other side and drop the handcuffs to the floor.

I feel my way around the dimly lit room. I know there has to be a door somewhere to get out of here. I hear a whimper to my right, but I can't see who it is.

I whisper to them, "I'll be back, I promise."

I touch the walls, noticing everything is concrete until I feel the handle, and I know this is the door. I open it a little, and it squeaks. I hold my breath, waiting and listening. When there is no movement, I walk through it and feel steps. Using my hands, I climb the steps up until they stop. I wait a few seconds with bated breath, hoping no one is here.

I can see some light shining through a window. I make my way toward the light, just making out a door underneath a window. I open the door, and the sun is shining brightly. I'm almost tempted to go back inside the building. It's too bright, it hurts my head.

"No, fight through this, Kim. You have to get back to Shelly and Declan," I tell myself. I shield my face from the sunlight, making out woods nearby. I don't know where I am, but I know I need to get into those woods and try to find my way home.

I take off running, with only the thoughts of Declan and Shelly pushing me. I can feel the mud, leaves, and sticks under my feet, but I keep going, praying I am going in the right direction and not in circles.

The day turned into night, but I didn't stop, I kept running, pushing myself, until one day, I ran into a barn. I see the hole, but I don't hear anything inside. My body hurts from the beating I've endured, the running I've been doing, for I don't know how many days, and I know I need to rest.

I climb through the whole and find an area out of sight. I lay on the floor and close my eyes. I don't know how long I slept, but when I wake, the sun is setting, as I can make out the last few minutes of daylight.

I climb back through the hole that I came in and run around the building. There is a cute farmhouse, and though it's dark inside, the property and land around it looks to be taken care of. I contemplate knocking on the door, but I don't know who lives there. What if it's the man who did this to me? No, I have to keep going. I need to find my way back home.

I continue running, still not knowing what direction I'm running in, but I allow my feet to keep moving.

"God, please help me get home," I say as I pray to the Lord above.

When I come out of the woods, I see a parking lot and a big building. It looks familiar, but it's dark, and I can't tell what it is. I run up, hoping to find a security guard or something, when all of a sudden, I see the big letters telling me this is the State Building.

"Oh God, Shelly," I call out, "Thank you God, thank you."

My feet keep moving until I'm in the building, and I know I'm safe once I'm in the elevator. I make it to Shelly's office, and I hear her scream before everything goes black.

"Hey, are you okay? Kim?" I hear Frankie say as I'm pulled from the memory.

I look around and see we are still on the road, surrounded by woods.

"Where are we?" I ask him.

"I'm not sure. Somewhere on the other side of Largo. GPS says we have ten more miles until we are at the destination. Are you okay?" he asks again.

"Yeah, I'm good."

"Where were you just then?" he asks.

"I think some of my memories are coming back," I tell him.

"Oh, like what?"

"Running through the woods," I say.

"That's great," he tells me as he places his hand on my thigh and squeezes.

"What are you doing?" I ask as I bat his hand away.

"I was just showing you support," he says with a frown.

"By putting your hand on my thigh?" I look at him incredulously.

"I'm sorry, I didn't mean anything by it," he says defensively.

"You should never put your hand on a woman's thigh without her permission," I scold him like he's a child.

"Damn, so touchy. I was just being nice," he says, and I can't tell if he's getting upset.

The GPS tells us we have arrived at our destination, but when I look around, I don't see Eric's car.

"What is going on? Where is Eric's car?" I ask.

"I don't know, maybe he parked on the opposite side of the building?" he says, not sounding convinced, but then shrugs his shoulders. "This is the location he sent me."

He steps out of the car, but I get a bad feeling, especially when I look at the building in front of me. It reminds me of the building I remembered with the window above the door.

I discreetly pull the phone Eric gave me from my pocket and send a location pin to Declan and Eric, then I dial Eric's number before sliding it into my jacket pocket, just in case this isn't what is supposed to happen.

I step out of the car and continue to look at the building in front of us.

"Maybe you should call Eric and find out where they are at?" I tell him.

He looks at his phone and says with a frown, "I have no cell service out here."

"How is that possible?" I ask. "Frankie, what the hell is going on?" I add, looking at him.

"I don't know," he whispers, "But maybe we should go inside and see if they are in there," he then suggests, and reluctantly, I follow him to the building.

As we walk up, my stomach is screaming at me to run. I look over at the woods, and wonder, not for the first time since my memory went, *is this the building I ran from?*

We walk inside, and there's not much in there. A dirty concrete floor and some type of black stacked pipes. This looks like it was used as some type of factory work, the pipes being for steam or fire maybe, I'm not sure.

We walk a little more ways in, and I say, "I don't hear anyone. Maybe we should leave and find a place to call Eric."

"I think you're right," Frankie says, and as we start to turn around, I hear.

"Welcome home, Kimberly," a voice says, causing my heart to beat with fear.

I never heard the man come up behind us. I don't know where he came from, and I can't help but immediately step back.

I hear Frankie gasp before saying, "It can't be?"

Chapter Twenty-Eight

KIM

I turn to look at Frankie, still keeping the man in front of my line of sight. "Do you know this man?" I ask him, but Frankie looks pale.

"Frankie?" I call out.

"Hello, son," the man says, and this time, it's my turn to gasp. "You've been a huge help these last ten years."

"What?" I ask, but Frankie hasn't moved. He just keeps staring at the man in front of us as if he's a ghost.

I look at the man in front of me, and I can see the resemblance in the facial features, but not the eyes. Frankie must have his mother's eyes. The eyes of the man in front of me are cold and cruel.

"You're dead," Frankie whispers.

"Oh, no, son. I never died," he laughs, that manic laugh that I remember. "Now your mother on the other hand." He chuckles.

"Where is my mom? What did you do to her?" Frankie yells out, and I can see his hands ball into fists.

"Still haven't found her, huh?" he says with glee. "No, of course you haven't. I don't imagine you are likely to either," he states simply, before turning his eyes back on me.

"I told you I'd have you back soon, and thanks to my son, here we are."

"It was you? You took Kim?" Frankie whispers in disbelief.

"Of course, I did," he says, never taking his eyes off me.

"Why? How?" he asks, and I want to know the answer too.

"Because you wanted her," he says simply. "As for the how, well I don't need to tell you everything."

Frankie looks at me apologetically before he lunges for his father.

I watch as Frankie knocks his father to the ground and punches him in the face over and over.

I never even see the knife until Frankie is stabbed in the stomach and he stops his assault on his father. His father pushes him off and gets up.

I look down at Frankie, mortified as his face goes pale, grabbing hold of the knife that is now protruding out of his stomach, close to his lungs.

He looks up at me with eyes so wide as he tries to breathe.

His father pulls the knife from his stomach, causing Frankie to scream out.

"ARGHHHH."

He kicks Frankie in the stomach. where he stabbed him as he says, "You are as pathetic as your mother, as all the cunts who you have managed to get to feel sorry for you," he spits at him.

Frankie is curled up in the fetal position. I can see the blood pooling around him, and his face is white. His father bends down and whispers something in his ear.

For a moment, I can see the fire and rage in Frankie's eyes as he looks at the man, who says loud enough, "But don't worry, you'll be dead soon, and they will be with me."

He laughs as he stands up, looking over at me.

"Come on, Kimberly, it's time to continue our game."

I can't help the fear that overtakes me. I'm frozen in my spot. My mind tells me to run, but my heart says I can't leave Frankie.

"Run, Kim, Run," Frankie croaks out, able to see my internal battle.

My eyes fill with tears as I turn and run, not knowing where I am going, or if there is another way out.

I hear the laugh of the madman behind me, but he's not running.

"There's nowhere to run to and nowhere to hide, Kimberly. The only way in and out is through the door you came in from. I've made sure of that."

I don't believe him, there has to be another way. I will not allow this man to hurt me again.

"No one is coming to save you. No one knows you are here," he sings out with glee.

I find a doorway, and I go through it into another room. There are stairs that lead up to what looks like it could have been an office. I don't think, I just run up them, needing a place to hide and get my bearings.

I go into the office and lock the door. There is a desk, but no phone. A standup cabinet and a wall of windows. I look to the right of me and see a bathroom that doesn't look to have been used in years.

I run to the windows and see I'm only two floors up. I try the latch on the window, and it won't move, then I see the nail. Looking down the line of windows, they are all nailed.

"This asshole really did think of everything," I mumble to myself.

I take in the chair that is next to the desk, and I look at the door. I know if I break the glass, he is going to hear it and will either break down the door or be outside before I can get back up after jumping.

"Damn, I wish I knew where he was at," I say to myself as I continue looking around. I pull the phone out of my pocket and see the blank screen. I don't know if Eric ever answered my call or if he hung up.

I try to dial his number again, but like with Frankie, there is no service. I don't know if they got my location pin or not.

"Damn," I say as I put the phone back in my pocket. I check the desk drawers for something sharp, anything to help defend myself.

The door knob rattles before I hear his sickly voice on the other side. "Kimberly, I'm getting a little bored with this game. Let's play my game."

I know time is running out. It won't be long before he breaks that door down to get in here. I have to make a decision now. I grab the chair, looking down at the ground from the window. There is nothing but grass and dirt, and I can see the woodline. If I can survive the fall without breaking anything and make it to the woods, I'm sure there is somewhere I can hide.

Just as I'm about to throw the chair through the glass, I hear the firing of a gun. Immediately, my instincts have me hitting the floor.

Where the hell did he get a gun from?

"Kim? Kim, are you in there?"

"Declan?" I whisper.

"Kim?" he calls as he turns the knob.

It can't be Declan. I must be hearing things. All of the sudden a body slams the door, like they are trying to break in. I know the door is old and won't hold for long. I get up off the floor and pick up the chair.

The door breaks as I throw the chair through the window.

"KIM, NO!" Declan screams out, as I'm about to jump from the window.

I freeze, shock taking over. I look over my shoulder and it is Declan. My shoulders sag with relief, but I look behind him expecting the man to show up.

"Kim," he calls my name softer as he breathes a sigh of relief, holding his hand out to me.

"Declan," I say, tears pooling in my eyes. "You found us," I tell him as he pulls me up into his arms.

"Yeah, baby, I found you, thanks to the location pin you dropped, but when I couldn't get you on the phone, I knew something was wrong."

"Where is he?" I ask, hearing the fear in my voice.

"We got him."

I cry into his chest, then I remember Frankie.

"Frankie," I say, pulling away from Declan.

"Mya and Heath are taking care of him," he tells me, and I finally allow my shoulders to relax.

Eric comes into the room and looks me up and down, making sure I'm okay.

"I'm okay, I promise, he didn't touch me," I tell them both before asking, "Is he..." I can't get it all out.

"No. I shot him in the shoulder," Declan says.

"I've got him handcuffed, Heath is watching over him, and backup should be here momentarily," Eric says.

"Who is he?" Declan asks, and to my surprise, it's Eric who answers.

"That's Frankie's father."

"How did you know?" I ask Eric, still clinging onto Declan like he's my lifeline.

"I read his file, as I have read all your files when you came to work for me," he says.

"Is he a serial killer?" Declan asks.

"Nothing in my files ever indicated as such, so I don't know?" Eric says, looking thoughtful.

"I swear I've seen him before, but I can't place where," Declan says, looking thoughtful.

"I don't understand, why would he kidnap me? What about the other person I heard?" I ask.

"What other person?" Declan asks.

"I remember the night I escaped. I couldn't see very well because of my swollen eyes, and the basement where I was at, the light was very dim. I managed to get out of the handcuffs, and as I made it to the door, I remember hearing a whimper. I promised whoever it was, I would be back to get them," I tell them both.

"We will find her, babe," Declan says. "For now, let's get you out of here and Frankie to the hospital."

We walk downstairs and back to the room where Frankie is currently lying passed out on the floor.

I look over at his dad. His shoulder is bleeding, but he will live. He is sitting on the floor, his hands cuffed behind his back, and Heath is standing over him.

"How did you get my number?" I ask.

"Why Frankie, of course," he says with a laugh and then says nothing else as he continues to laugh.

I look over at Frankie, who is passed out and very pale. He has lost a lot of blood.

"What about the other girl? Where is she?" I ask.

"What other girl?" he asks, looking sincerely confused.

I don't have time to ask anything more as the state troopers arrive as well as the EMTs. The EMTs load Frankie onto a stretcher to get him to the hospital.

The troopers lift his dad up and walk him to their car. They will drive him to the hospital and have him looked at before they book him in the state jail.

When they open the door, he turns and looks at me. "Kimberly, we aren't done yet. There is still so much more to learn, so many dreams to be had," he says as he laughs that manic laugh.

The troopers put him in the car, but I can't help the shiver that spreads through my body.

"What's going to happen to him?" I ask.

"He'll be charged with kidnapping a federal agent and attempted murder of another. That should put him away for a long time," Eric says.

"Let's get to the hospital and check on Frankie," Declan says as Eric and I stand there watching the car pull away.

Heath comes up and pulls me into his arms, "Girl, don't you ever scare me like that again. I thought we lost you, especially after..." he gets quiet, then finishes, "After we saw Frankie lying there."

I pull back and tell him, "I didn't mean to scare you."

"What brought you two out here anyway?" Mya asks.

"Frankie, he said you texted him this location and wanted us both here," I say as I look at Eric.

"I didn't send a text to Frankie," Eric says, sounding mystified.

"Boss, I have Frankie's phone right here, and it says you did, with a pin to this location," Mya tells us.

"He wasn't lying," I whisper. "How is that possible?" I ask Eric.

"I don't know." He looks at all of us and shakes his head. "But we will find out," he adds with determination on his face.

We all head to the car. Heath and Mya take the one Frankie and I came in, and I ride with Eric and Declan in theirs.

We get to the hospital to find Frankie is currently in surgery, so we are instructed to wait in the waiting room for the doctor to come out.

Shelly comes running into the emergency room. "Oh, thank God," she says when she sees me and pulls me in for a big hug. "Are you okay?"

"Yeah, I'm fine, but Frankie isn't," I tell her.

"I know, but he will be," she says as she sits down in between Eric and I, while Declan is on my other side, rubbing small circles on my back.

I don't know if he realizes he's doing it, but since I need his touch more than I need to pretend we have no relationship, I say nothing as we all continue to wait together.

Five hours later, the doctor comes out to tell us Frankie made it through surgery. They had to repair a perforation in his lung and his intestines, but with plenty of rest, he should recover nicely.

<hr />

Three weeks later

We all make our way to the hospital to check on Frankie as we do every night, before going home. I have a bag of food from his favorite fast food place, McDonald's.

We walk in, and he's sitting up in bed, looking so much better.

"Hey, Frankie, how are you feeling?" I ask, handing him his bag.

"Better now that there is food," he says as his eyes light up.

"Boy, you are going to turn into a Big Mac if you keep eating those," Heath says.

"It beats the food they serve here. No flavor whatsoever," he says as he takes a bite of the Big Mac.

"Any news on..." he can't bring himself to call that man his father, and now I understand why.

Frankie watched his father beat his mother until one night, she disappeared. His father told him she was weak and left. Didn't want to be with them anymore.

Frankie couldn't believe she would leave without taking him with her. His dad started bringing home different women. Some would have bruises on them like his mother used to. He remembers one night, his father tried to get him to beat a woman, but he refused, so his father beat the woman in front of him until she couldn't move.

He always assumed the women left just like his mother, but when he joined the FBI ten years ago, he went searching for his mom. He still hasn't found her and now he's wondering if his father killed his mother.

Eric is looking into how Frankie received a text from him that he never sent. Cyber security is investigating, and hopefully they will be able to tell us something soon.

We are also still looking into who the woman I heard could be. Though Frankie's father said there was no one, I know I heard some-one. Declan and I have been scouring the missing person's reports. Looking for anything that may resemble how I was taken or someone who received phone calls and may have filed a report. So far, we have hit a brick wall, but that doesn't mean we will quit searching.

"No, he's still in the state jail awaiting trial. No date has been set yet, likely waiting for you to be released from the hospital so you can testify," Eric tells him, and Frankie nods.

"I'll definitely be glad to get out of here. I'm sorry you had to spend so long here," he tells me.

I give him a small smile. "It does suck, doesn't it?"

Everyone laughs, including Frankie.

"Well, the plus side is the nurses are pretty spectacular here," he says, giving me a wink, and I can only shake my head.

"You are definitely getting better," Heath says, shaking his own head.

"Frankie finishes his dinner, then sighs before looking at me. "So are you going to tell us?"

I look at him, confused, then look around the room to see if anyone knows what he's talking about. Everyone but Declan, who is standing behind me, is looking at me.

"What?" I ask.

He sighs again. "Are you two dating?" he asks as he points to Declan and I.

"Yes," I say, with no hesitation whatsoever.

"I knew it," Heath says, looking pointedly at Declan.

"Yeah, I thought so too," Frankie says quietly.

I look over at Eric and see him assessing Frankie.

"If it's a problem, I have no issues with transferring back to the DC office so as not to disrupt the team dynamics," I tell everyone, and I feel Declan stiffen behind me.

"And we end up with someone else, hell no," Heath says.

"No, it's not an issue. I think I've known for a long time that you two were meant for each other," Frankie says, shaking his head. "I just kind of hoped you would choose me."

"Frankie, I love you like a brother,"

"An annoying one," Heath mutters and Mya elbows him.

But I continue on. "Always have, always will, but it was never going to be more than that," I tell him softly.

"I know, I get it," he says, and I can see he does.

We all say good night and head back home.

Later that night, Declan and I are woken up by the ringing of the phone.

"Could you get that, please," I call out before Declan turns the bedside lamp on and answers his phone.

"Boss, what's wrong?"

I immediately sit up in bed. Worry for Michelle hitting me.

"What? When?"

God, why won't he put the phone on speaker so I can hear what Eric is saying?

"We will be there in a few minutes," he says, hanging up.

"What is it?" I ask.

"Frankie's gone."

"What? How?"

"We don't know yet. Eric wants us at the hospital to view video footage and find out."

"Shit," I say, pulling on some leggings and a t-shirt, throwing my hair in a bun, slipping on tennis shoes before running out the door.

Coming Soon

Want to know what happened to Frankie?

DREAM TO MURDER

Book Four

Will be coming in 2025

Cover Reveal and Preorder Alert coming soon.

Acknowledgements

I want to thank everyone who has been with me during this entire journey. This month is two years since I have been an author, and you all are the reason why. Your faith, love, and support in me is what pushes me to continue to allow my mind to conjure up these stories. I would not be here today without you all and I want you to know I love you very much.

I want to especially thank Kerrie, Mikki, my three lovely Beta readers, Carli, Dawn, and Dianne. Angel, Renea, and Krissy, without you all my books wouldn't be as good as they are.

I want to thank the ARC team as well, if not for you being with me on this journey, no one would read my books and without your reviews, shares, and support, I would not be where I am. Thank you all very much.

To the readers who find this series, thank you for taking a chance and reading. If you loved it, please leave a review and let your friends know.

xxx,

Bella Lane

About the author

I'm an author of steamy suspenseful romance novels, who loves to keep her readers guessing.

I have always loved the idea of happy endings, but with real life drama.

I currently live in North Carolina and have always loved the beauty of the Appalachian Mountains. Hiking is one of my favorite hobbies as it helps to clear my mind and allow my imagination to roam freely.

I'm an avid reader of all genres.

I love traveling, especially to small communities, as the people are always so nice and welcoming, with hidden gems in their sweet little towns.

Come follow me to learn more.

Facebook Reader Group – https://www.facebook.com/groups/436971591638212

Instagram – https://www.instagram.com/author_bella_lane/

Website – https://www.bellalanebooks.com

Also by

BELLA LANE

Men of Special Ops Forces

Stroke of Midnight (Roman and Jessi's story)

Driving Home for Christmas (Nico and Sarah's story)

His Christmas Baby (Jonathan and Shawna's story)

A Soldier's Secret Romance (Ryan and Ellie's story)

Saved by the Major (Noah and Amanda's story)

Claiming Homebase (Justin and Livia's story)

Finding Ireland (Liam and Ireland's story)

The General's Secret (Connor and Destiny's story)

Top Grunt Services Series

Protected by the Bodyguard (Scott and Brianne's story)

Falling for the Bodyguard (Brody and Cami's story)

Loving the Bodyguard (Jax and Lena's story)

Shielded by the Bodyguard (Matt and Alisa's story)

Heroes of Maine Series

Defending Charley (Derrick and Charlene's story)

Saving Sam (Connor and Samantha's story)

Protecting Leia (Noah and Leia's story)

Healing the Quarterback (Will and Krista's story)

Saving St. Nicolas (Mike and Riley's story)

His Curvy Surprise

Behavioral Unit Maine Series

Run To Murder

Train To Murder

Milton Keynes UK
Ingram Content Group UK Ltd.
UKHW020340081124
450874UK00011B/603